Death at Little Mound

Linda Tassel Mysteries Book 1

by Eileen Charbonneau

Print ISBNs
Amazon Print 978-0-2286-1752-5
LSI Print 978-0-2286-1753-2
B&N Print 978-0-2286-1754-9

BWL Publi...

Books we love to write ...
Authors around the world.

http://bwlpublishing.ca

Dedication

My thanks to Clan Mother Phyllis Lay for welcoming me onto the reservation and into her life, Juilene McKnight for providing my passport, and Linda Morris for befriending a lonely Buffalo soul in Georgia

Chapter One
Summer, 1992

Tad Gist looked down at the girl crouching in the trench. He became lost in the swirling red pattern of the kerchief tied around her black hair. With a dry paint brush and infinite patience, she dusted around the small skull of the skeleton. How could she do that, staying so still in that deep gash in the Georgia clay, brushing dirt off bones? Then she began to sing. He listened closely to the soft, crooning melody, maybe a lullaby. He didn't understand the words.

Suddenly, Tad saw the wall of dirt beside the girl breaking up, caving in. She reached over to protect the bones. Tad reached down for the girl's arm. He had to help her—

She turned, looked up at him, and smiled.

"Hey! Haul some of this dirt out?"

Tad blinked. The image of the cave-in disaster was gone.

"Uh, sure."

Phew. He had to stop playing "Escape from Demon Lair" on his computer. He grabbed the handle of the bucket the girl held up to him.

"You wearing sun block?" the girl asked.

"No."

"You'd better put some on." She shielded her eyes and made a soft, clicking sound. "You don't even have a farmer's tan."

"A farmer's—?"

"Just arms and neck."

She was right. Watching TV and playing computer games since his family's move to the South hadn't contributed to his color. Or his conversation skills.

He shrugged. "I guess I have a Buffalo tan."

"Buffalo?" She tilted her head. "But that would be very dark, to be like the buffalo."

Tad smiled. "The city, not the animal. I'm from Buffalo, New York. Plenty of snow. Not a lot of sun."

"Oh!" Her beaded quill earrings danced. He was the opposite of this compact, laughing girl whose bronze tone brimmed with health. "Are you not the assistant Dr. Hamilton promised me?"

She thought he was some college guy? Cool. "No. I'm just visiting. With my father. Morris University's new anthropologist. He's touring the site, then collecting the weekly base camp reports to bring back to Atlanta."

She looked disappointed that he was not the guy she was expecting. Or was he imagining that? "Well, come down into the shade, Buffalo Man. We put even our visitors to work."

She held the wooden ladder steady.

Tad looked around frantically, trying to think of an excuse not to climb down into that trench—one that wouldn't make him sound like a wimp or a jerk. Or crazy with visions of being buried alive.

Inspiration didn't strike. He descended.

The suddenly cooler temperature of the dig site made him feel clammy. The trench widened into a cavernous chamber about the side of his bedroom. He caught a peripheral view of a skeleton on its stone bier, a string of copper beads across its ribcage.

He didn't want to look directly at those bones, or let go of the girl's offered hand go. So he shook it.

"I'm Tad. My father's Dr. Stan Gist, My mother's Kelsey Doyle. She just got a job at Current News Network. That's why we moved here. Well, Atlanta. We live in Atlanta, near the university. What's that? Abut ninety miles south of here? I was half asleep in the car."

Let go, let go of her, he told his grasping fingers. Either all you can do is grunt, or else you can't shut up.

But now it was the girl who was holding on, giving his hand a firm shake.

"I am Linda, daughter of Naomi, Ani-Waya clan mother. My father is James

Tassel. We live near Cartersville." She released his hand. Her earrings danced again to the rhythm of her laugh. "We are formal down here in the mud!"

Linda looked at the skeleton. "This is my friend, whom I call Tallalla."

Tad forced himself to look at the bones on the slab of concave rock. The small skeleton was not laid out flat, but huddled as if cold, knees toward chest. The feet crossed over each other almost gracefully. The finger bones of one hand rested on the opposite shoulder. The skull was hardest to investigate—the deep eye sockets, the jaw dropped open in what seemed to Tad like an everlasting scream. "Tallalla," he said. "What does that mean?"

"Woodpecker. Because I believe she was a pipe stem carver—an artist who needs to peck with very hard hammers to find her vision in the stone."

"But wasn't this a child?"

"No. Tallalla is a woman. The people of this land were smaller then, five hundred years before Columbus landed. Does your father not tell you about the Mound Builders here at the dig?"

"Oh, sure. I forgot that part," he said, too quickly. Since his family had made the decision to relocate, he hadn't wanted to hear about anything—his parents' jobs, or the high school he'd be entering as a stranger in the fall. Because of them.

8

Because his father was more interested in the long dead than his own family. Because his mother had "outgrown" Buffalo and wanted a shot at a bigger TV market.

"The Mound Builders were of the culture the scientists call Mississippian," Linda continued. "The big, spectacular mounds are mostly in the Midwest. Here in Georgia, archeologists have already done extensive work at the Etowah site. I guess that's why most didn't think these mounds were worth preserving when the dam project came up." Her arms opened in a graceful, helpless gesture. "'Seen one outpost of ancient Mississippian civilization, seen them all,' was the attitude, before Morris University stepped in. We are so grateful, Tad."

Yes. Tad remembered about the time constraints brought on by the dam project. That was one of the reasons his family had to move so quickly. He felt the anger return to stiffen his arms, flush his face. Control it. This girl had nothing to do with his family's move, he told himself. But her commitment to the project was causing a metallic taste in his mouth.

Linda turned to the skeleton. "Tallalla was buried in a fashion that befits a craftsperson," she said. "I found tools at her head, and many ceremonial pipe stems around her. They were carved in the forms of the frog, the owl, the turtle—see?" She took up a sketchbook full of accurate, detailed pencil drawings of pottery shards, small bowls, and the skeleton itself, at various stages of unearthing. Toward the back of the book she flipped to renderings of the carved pipe stems. The collection went beyond good craftsmanship, Tad realized. Linda Tassel was an artist.

"The pipe stems are not like the ones found at other gravesites," she explained. "Those are all different, created by different carvers. These were done by one, I think. Maybe when this woman died they buried her with some of her own work. Do you think that makes sense, Tad?"

"Sure, why not?"

Tad frowned at his own inability to say something more intelligent to this wonderfully talented, articulate, girl. But his few words brought a bright smile to her face. "Why not, exactly!" "Dr. Duncan, he says those are the words of a dreamer, not a scientist. My 'speculative leaps,' as he calls them, have—"she made her voice more nasal and strident—"'too high an imagination level.' But Dr. Steffy does not always agree. Neither does Dr. Hamilton. And he is Dig Boss."

Linda bit her lip and an awkward silence intruded before she smiled brightly. "Tad. I don't know that name. Are you a good swimmer, then? Named after the tadpole?"

"No!" The word blared, even though the red clay walls blunted some of its force.

"What does it mean?" she persisted quietly.

Tad ran his hand through blond hair in need of a trim. "It's short for Taddeusz."

"Taddeusz," she pronounced carefully. "How exotic!"

A girl with her head wrapped in a red turban and wearing porcupine quills hanging off her ears was calling him exotic? But he swallowed a rejoinder when he realized that she was intrigued, not being mean. "It's not exotic in my old neighborhood," he explained.

"In Buffalo?"

"Yeah. East side of the city. It's Polish. My grandfather had his last name shortened by the paymaster of his steel plant after he immigrated from Poland, way back. Dad's family's been making up for it in fancy first names ever since."

Linda laughed. "I like that tradition. And the meaning?"

"Well, Taddeusz is the Polish form of Thaddeus. It means 'courageous,'"

"I like that, too."

She meant it. Maybe it was not so bad to be exotic, Tad thought. Linda's dark eyes took on the brightness of polished stone as she lowered her voice to a shared-secret tone. "Look what I found today, Tad." She took a bundle from a recess in the wall, then carefully unwrapped a soapstone carving from a yellow bandana. It fit neatly into the palm of her hand. "A human face. Do you think it might be Tallalla herself?"

He took the green-tinged stone in his hands, then turned it slowly to catch all the angles. The face had a broad forehead and prominent cheekbones. The chin was small and pointed, like Linda Tassel's own. And the carved woman had something, maybe deerskin, wrapped around her head. Tad sensed a warm, serene beauty from the stone. Linda was right, a gifted artist had crafted the image. Linda's own drawings were wonderful, she would recognize another artist. "You sound like you know her," he said.

"I have been living at her gravesite for three summers now." Her bright eyes dimmed. "This will be the last, now that the river is being flooded. Did your father explain that?"

Tad nodded, wishing his own attention span had been more generous toward his father and his enthusiasm toward the Mound Builders dig. But he remembered about the flooding, because it meant his own future was a victim, too.

All of his plans were in ruins. At Roosevelt High he had gone from JV to Varsity volleyball in winter, baseball in spring. He'd worked well with the coaches, helped them form championship potential teams. The school's volleyball had made it to the sectionals, baseball to the finals last season. Tad had been voted captain of each for his senior year— the year they were going for state championships, the year of his senior prom, to which he'd already asked Judy Tolliver. The year he'd now never have at Roosevelt.

"I guess I get carried away," Linda apologized, taking the carvings from him and replacing them in the soft cloth.

"No! I mean, sure you do, but I think it's great, your enthusiasm."

Stupid. The move to this dense Georgia heat was making him stupid, atrophied his brain.

Linda's smile returned. "Tell me how you feel about my enthusiasm after you do some more dirt hauling, Buffalo Man."

Together, they carried the rest of the buckets to the surface.

"Should I dump this dirt over—"Tad began, reaching for the handles of a red wheelbarrow close by.

"Oh, no!"

At the sound of alarm in her voice, something came to growling life from the shade of the wheelbarrow—a black and white dog. Part hound, part Labrador retriever, maybe some sheepdog in the mix. The dog leapt to Linda's side, the fur on his back and tail standing up. He barked fiercely.

"Foolish Boy, hush! No! *Kwa!*"

The dog obeyed Linda, but stood protectively, his head against her hip. Upon her nod, Tad placed his opened hand beneath the dog's mouth. The animal sniffed, then licked Tad's fingers.

"Wow, his tongue is dry."

"Foolish Boy shows that sign of his ancestor. *Waya*, the wolf."

"*Waya*, Tad repeated. "Your mother's clan name."

"Yes. And mine. The Principle People are matrilineal."

"Principle People?"

"The *Tsa la ki*. You call us the Cherokee."

"Oh, sure." Wow. Linda was an Indian, like the people she was digging up. He'd seen *Dances With Wolves* three times two summers ago. Those Indians were cool. Tad searched his mind for something smart to say. "Don't you people belong in Oklahoma?"

Linda's lips became a tight line. "We belong here. Though most of us were driven west on our Trail of Tears, in the last century. Some hid in the mountains from the soldiers. I am descended from those who stayed, part of the Eastern Nation."

Tad knew his smile was lame. "My grandparents were from Poland, remember? And my mom's people are 1900s-wave Irish. They dug the New York city subways. None of us fought Indians. Or met any before today." He exhaled. "That's no excuse for my ignorance. I'm sorry."

Linda cocked her head, grinned. "Good thing your ancestors were so late coming over."

"Why?"

Her smile broadened as she surveyed the disheveled blonde curls hanging over his forehead. "Nice hair," she said malevolently.

His scalp prickled even as he joined her laughter.

Foolish Boy barked. In a playful tone, Tad hoped. Linda took a leathery beef jerky stick from her pocket and handed it to Tad. "Here," she told him, "seal your friendship."

Foolish Boy lapped up the treat with his dry tongue, whining happily in appreciation as Linda approached the wheelbarrow.

"This must be sifted, down at base camp," she explained.

"Why? It's just dirt."

"But it might still hold treasures. It needs to go through metal mesh. It takes two people, one to shake the sifter, the other to stand by to remove large stones and clumped clay that might damage tiny, delicate objects."

Tad made a face. "Sounds like trying to find a needle in a haystack."

"Exactly. And a lot dirtier. Not my favorite task."

"I'll help," Tad offered.

She narrowed her eyes. "Sifting? Or hauling?"

Tad remembered complaining to his father about everything—from getting up early that morning for the two-hour ride to the dig site, to the bumpy back roads.

"Both," he said now, and meant it.

Linda climbed back down into the dig site and removed soil from under the saucer-like rock that was the ancient Indian's bier. Tad filled the wheelbarrow with buckets that she handed up to him. Sometimes she disappeared completely under the rock's protection. Protection. Tad remembered the frightening image of Linda's own burial. It seemed so real, even now. He shook the image away.

When they finished their task, Tad helped Linda cover her trench with a bright yellow tarp, then anchor it down with nearby rocks.

Linda Tassel seemed smaller on the surface. She barely reached Tad's chin. Her dig site was on the lonely lower outskirts of the three larger mounds. Its remoteness had drawn Tad to the site for a walk after his latest argument with his father...

"Your best grades are in history, Tad," his father had said as they toured the dig site. "Don't you even want to walk around, see it come alive?"

"Dug up by people who didn't get to play in their sandboxes enough when they were kids? No, thanks."

"Planning to major in armchair pop psychology in college?"

"If I go to college."

"What are you talking about? Of course you'll be going to—"

"I don't have to. I'm almost eighteen. I don't even have to finish high school down here with a bunch of southern hicks."

He saw his father's neck flush red and knew he was out of patience. "You're right, Tad. You don't have to do anything, anything at all. I'll come looking for you in an hour or two."

Then he'd left Tad standing there in the burning sun on the outskirts of the site.

Tad hadn't meant it, not any of it. How could he make things right?

Linda fisted her hands at her waist and looked over two baskets of numbered artifacts, each wrapped carefully in one of her colorful kerchiefs. Tad felt his frown fading. He'd much rather look at her than think of his argument with his father.

Although Linda's own bandana kerchief was wrapped around her head in what Tad imagined was a traditional Indian fashion, the rest of her was in the usual fashion of archeological digs...worn cut-off jean shorts and a sleeveless ribbed knit cotton shell top. Tad felt his shirt plastered to his back with sweat. If he dressed like Linda, he'd get a burn that would quickly bake his hide to well-done level. But he didn't mind the look on her at all.

"First stop—infirmary," she said.

"Infirmary?"

"Where the sun block is."

"Oh, yeah."

He reached down, taking the handles of the wheelbarrow. As Linda walked beside him, carrying her baskets, he saw the muscles of her upper arms flex powerfully. Best stay on her good side. He wondered if she played ball. This girl must have a great swing.

Linda led the way down to base camp, talking over her shoulder as she went. As other workers nodded and greeted them, Tad did not quite feel the outsider walking beside her, even in his heavy jeans and sweaty, rolled up, shirtsleeves.

"Sister!"

Beyond a tent, a guy standing with a group of demonstrators holding home-made placards caught Tad's attention. And stopped Linda.

A large Indian guy a few years older than Tad came forward. He had a group of three other guys in sunglasses standing around him like an entourage. "Why do you defile the resting place of our ancestors?" he shouted out.

Linda slowly put down her baskets. Foolish Boy trotted quickly to her right side.

Tad released to wheelbarrow and stood at her left.

He watched Linda's face grow somber, but remain serene. "The bones of the Mound Builders talk," she responded, "before the damming of the Allatoona quiets them forever."

"Who is listening? Whites and apple Indians, unmindful of our ways! You are hastening our defeat, I think."

"I am salvaging what I can, with respect. It may be we take different paths to the same place, my brother."

"Careful, Ahyoka," a demonstrator in a fringed vest called out after looking over the items in her baskets. "They will put a number on you and add you to their museum."

The big guy frowned but the others laughed. Tad watched disapproval from another demonstrator, an old woman with a kerchief wound around her head in the same fashion as Linda's. She chastised them in a harsh version of the language that sounded like Linda's lullaby. Of course, Tad realized, it was the Cherokee language. He'd never thought of Native Americans having their own languages, besides the halting, grunting English or fierce war cries of old Western movies, before he'd seen the dubbed Indian language in *Dances With Wolves*.

Linda's hands made white knuckled fists around the handles of her baskets, but her serene expression didn't change. She turned and walked on as if nothing had happened, Foolish Boy at her side.

"Linda," Tad called, catching up. "Wait!"

She didn't turn. "Come on. You will start to burn."

"I'm burning now! Do you know that guy? The one in the vest?"

"Yes. His name is Guli Whitepath. He and I dance together on festival days. He lives in the Qualla Boundary, the Cherokee reservation to the north of here. He makes beautiful glassware, ceremonial hoops, and forges knives." She sighed. "And he's angry with me for being part of the dig."

"Aren't you angry? With him and his pals, I mean? Didn't they insult you?"

"Insult me? How?"

"One called you a name! A—Ayoga?"

"Ahyoka," she corrected. That is my name. My Cherokee name."

"Oh." Tad realized he was falling behind her quick steps, and caught up. "What's an apple Indian?"

"An Indian who acts white. You know— red on the outside, white on the inside?"

Tad only caught a quick glimpse of her troubled eyes, she was moving so fast. "So? Isn't that an insult?"

"My mother is Snowbird Cherokee. The Snowbird had no intermarriage with whites until the 1960s. I have more of the blood of our ancestors than that one does, but blood quantum was imposed on us by the colonizers, and has led to trouble ever since. I'm an apple Indian in his eyes, because sometimes I act white, when I think it toward the common good."

"Even when the common good puts you in danger?"

Linda finally stopped and turned. Tad almost ran into her.

"What did that guy Guli mean? That part about 'hastening our defeat?' What does it mean?"

"There was a Cherokee protest over the flooding of this land for the dam," Linda explained. "We did not win. But then the university sponsored this dig, so that the life of the Mound Builders is not all lost. This land has not belonged to the Cherokee for many generations," she continued. "Still, they come down from Qualla Boundary, and from Snowbird, to protest. I admire their persistence, though I do not think the dam project will shut down. Only something extraordinary, some extraordinary find might do that."

"What about Tallalla? She's important, extraordinary, isn't she?"

"Oh, Tad." The words came out of her like a sigh. Was she pulling rank on him out here, in the bright sunlight? Wasshe finally seeing him like the ignorant seventeen-year-old he was? No. A pride shone in her eyes as she reached up, touched his shoulder. "It would have to be something of value to white people, I mean." He felt the demonstrators' eyes on them. Especially Guli's. "I'm not in any danger," Linda said with quiet assurance. "These are my people."

Tad shrugged, tried to smile. What did he know about any of this? "Maybe I'm getting sunstroke already, eh?"

She looked into the piercing blue sky, then shook her head. "Come on."

Then she noticed he was empty-handed. She pointed behind them with her delicate chin. "Go back and get the wheelbarrow, Buffalo Man. I'm still holding you to your sifting promise."

Chapter Two

When they ducked into the infirmary, the air was permeated by the citrus smell of sun block that Dr. Stan Gist was applying liberally to his arms. Seeing Tad, he jumped to his feet. When did that worried look become his immediate reaction, Tad wondered with a twinge of guilt.

"Tad! I was just coming to look for you," his father said. "Do you know these Mound Builders were buried with teeth of grizzly bears from the Rocky Mountains and obsidian from Central America? What a trading network!"

Tad winced at his father's nervous energy. Had their last exchange been so bad that he was now anticipating a flash of temper?

"Yeah, Dad," he said quietly. "Some network."

Dr. Gist's shoulders slumped. "I was so fascinated I forgot the time, son. I'm sorry."

Tad smiled. "Didn't anybody warn you that putting on the sun block means you've committed to a full day's work?"

"What?"

"Tad turned. "Isn't that right, Linda? Linda Tassel, this is my father, Dr. Stan Gist."

Linda smiled, nodding. "That's the deal, Dr. Gist. Looks like both of you are in for some sifting, while I load my data into the computer. You may be able to plead ignorance, of course, but Tad cannot."

"Stan can't either." A blond woman in a light khaki dress appeared from behind a makeshift wooden room divider. "I told him the same thing, Linda, so he promised to talk Tad into—"

"Not 'talk into', I didn't say 'talk into,'" Dr. Gist insisted.

"I'm Rose LaVetra, Tad," the woman said, holding out her hand, "chief medical officer of this time travel expedition."

Tad folded his arms. "It's a conspiracy, Dad. Women stick together. Just like Mom and Maggie at home."

"Maggie?" Linda asked.

"My little sister. She's seven."

Linda smiled. "Well, at least you are used to it."

Tad squeezed the white lotion on his exposed arms, hands and neck.

Astonishment lit his dad's features. Linda got a look of gratitude as well. "Dr. Hamilton speaks very highly of you, young woman."

Young woman? Oh, brother. Was he thinking that Linda wasn't in his league, and too old for him? And was she?

Linda grinned. "Dr. Hamilton knows a good bargain, sir. I'm supervisor, soil sampler, and artifact interpreter in my own little corner of the mound."

"Well, for now you're the boss of two assistants, with Dr. LaVetra's permission?"

His father waited for the doctor's nod, just as Tad had seen him do with his mother and many female colleagues.

He got it.

"Lead on," he told Linda.

* * *

Tad was glad he wasn't doing the sifting alone. Once he and his dad established a routine, the endless repetition of shaking out two feet by two feet square of wood and mesh to scan red Georgia clay clumps for artifacts could have been mind numbing.

"What are we looking for, Dad?"

"We can hope for a figurine, a piece of a knife, bone, earring, or pottery shard that Linda missed. Anything that looks man-made or interesting."

"And if we find something?"

"It goes to the field lab for formal study—where someone tries to determine its use, the source of manufacture, its distribution in the context of the tell."

25

"Tell. The site, you mean?"

"That's right."

"Dad?"

"Hmmn?"

Talk, Tad commanded a voice stressed by bad habits in his father's company. "Explain more about this place."

"What do you want to know?"

"Let's start with the bulldozers outside its limits. And the people protesting."

"I didn't think you were awake enough to notice either when we drove in this morning."

"I wasn't sleeping. I was…sulking."

His father's sandy mustache quivered. "The bulldozers belong to Peterson Construction—the dam builders," he said. "It's sad to think that the mounds of a thousand-year-old culture—a culture that withstood death, war, famine and the coming of the Europeans—will, by this time next year, be under water. The bulldozers are already working on the outskirts of the dig.

"The protestors are a mix—some local people who don't want the character of their home changed, environmentalists who say the lake will put the ecosystem out of balance, and of course, the Cherokee and their supporters. They claim the mound builders as their ancestors and don't want burial grounds to be flooded. Dr. Hamilton says the county sheriff's department has been keeping a close eye on them for signs of 'outside agitators.'" He sighed. "They don't understand that we are the outsiders."

"Linda said that the Cherokee tried to stop the dam."

"Yeah, and that was a losing cause from the start. See, the dam's a 'gift' from Mr. Peterson himself—privately financed after he bought up the land three years ago. No tax dollars, lots of local jobs, both with the construction, then afterward when the lake draws tourists. Most of the protestors are Cherokee, some not even residents of this state. That didn't stand in their favor either."

"Why are they mad at the university?"

"Some, because we're disturbing the dead. Others don't think much of us putting the old ones and their culture behind glass museum displays. Linda's brave, isn't she, to have stayed with the dig, with so many of her own people's disapproving?"

"Yeah."

"Her family has status among the Snowbird Cherokee. Though they're traditionalists, they have a native art and craft business that links them with life off the reservation, and brings in money to the community. They're trusted. I guess she's used to having a foot in each culture."

Returning workers passed them. Some nodded toward his father.

"Do these people live on-site, Dad?"

"All summer. They're putting in extra hours with Peterson breathing down our necks. He could cut us off and get us out at any time."

"And they're all specialists, like you? With advanced degrees and all?"

"Oh, no. They're all committed to the project, of course. But there is a fair share of hard-working amateurs on this site, just as on most archeological digs. I mean 'amateur' in its original sense, Tad—someone who works out of passion, love. Not for money."

Were the ones nodding to his father and casting a gimlet eye on him questioning his ability and passion, Tad wondered? One of them was looking up from his clipboard, frowning. Was he doing something wrong, lulled by the task's repetitiveness?

"What if I miss something? Maybe you'd better re-check what I've—"

"It's all right, son. Let the artifacts find you."

Tad made a face. "My father—Zen anthropologist," he teased.

His father laughed his funny, half wheeze chuckle. When was the last time he'd heard that? He missed the sound.

Continuing their search through the dirt, Tad picked out a clump of stubborn Georgia clay that formed a rough, four- or five-centimeter sphere. It was like a dozen others too big to get through the sifter. They'd been consigned to a heap. Tad lifted this one out to toss but stopped. It felt different. Heavier. His dad raised his head.

"Find something?"

"I don't know. The heft is different. And there's a ridge of some sort coming through."

"Save it for washing." Dr. Gist pointed to a box of small clear-plastic bags. "That's part of the system—everything suspicious has to be washed. If there's something within the clay, it will be labeled, then classified as to type, location, thickness, and function."

Tad cast a longing look at the trailer. "All that? Linda's already got two baskets of those broken pots and things."

"Artifacts, Tad."

"Right. Artifacts. Can I wash the one I found?"

"Sure."

"So, if it's nothing, well, nobody has to know."

"I don't think it's 'nobody' you're concerned about."

It was his father's turn to tease. Tad couldn't remember the last time his dad had felt free enough to engage him in this kind of banter. Tad put the clump of dirt into a plastic bag and shoved it into his jeans' pocket. "Have you seen Linda's drawings, Dad?"

"Dr. Hamilton showed me a number of them, yes. She's a very talented and hard-working young lady."

"So, what would she see in me, right?"

"I didn't say that."

"Sorry. I'm just thinking, maybe she'll get so busy in there—"

"She'll be out. And when she does, I think I'll ask her if she'd like an extra set of parents."

Tad frowned. "I don't need another sister."

"Stepsister. You can date a stepsister."

Tad felt himself coloring at his father's suggestion. The heat crept up his neck, like it always did on his father. "My Polish weather vanes," his mom called them.

"Dad, do you suppose Linda... I mean, would she think I was too young to, you know, interest her?"

His father ginned, but before he could answer, a man in a red checkered shirt and a pipe in his hand approached them. His father introduced the guy as Dr. Michael Steffy, the dig's geologist.

"Any luck?" he asked them.

"Only—"Tad reached into his pocket as Dr. Steffy crouched beside the sifter.

"Now this is interesting," he said.

Tad released his hold on his clump of clay and crouched beside him. There was nothing but fine soil on the tarp beneath the sifter, His fingers were examining it closely. "What, Dr. Steffy?"

"This soil. Unusual amounts of iron, some micas, vermiculites, if I'm not mistaken. You were working with Linda Tassel at Little Mound, weren't you?"

Word traveled fast, Tad thought. "That's right, sir."

"Where did this soil come from? Were you up top? Making the opening wider?"

"No. We were digging under the stone platform where Tall—"Tad checked himself, wondering if Dr. Steffy knew that Linda had named her skeleton woman. "Where the bones are laid out," he amended.

"Well, that's odd."

"How, Michael?" his father questioned Dr. Steffy.

"Well, let me ask you, Tad. Did the bones of Linda's lady look in any way disturbed?"

"No, sir. The skeleton fit on that stone dish like it was made for her. And the pipe-stems around her, and the copper necklace. It was all so dignified."

Dr. Steffy laughed. "A mystery, then."

"What is? Linda hasn't done anything wrong, has she? I mean, that's impossible, it must have been me."

"No, no." The man placed his hand on Tad's shoulder. He usually hated when his father's academic friends did that, like he was a sorry sub-species of *homoerectus* or something. But this one had calloused, workman fingers, even though he smelled of cherry pipe tobacco. "Let me test the soil. Don't mention this to Linda, it might be easily explained." He ran a small amount of the sifted soil through his fingers. "Sounds like you've got the archeology bug, Tad. Or are

31

you just taking perverse teen-aged delight in making a liar out of your father?"

"Sir?"

Dr. Steffy turned to his colleague. "'No interest' indeed, Stan! Why, the boy's a natural field worker. Those are excellent observations on the first day out. Give me one of those plastic bags, will you, Tad?"

Tad did. Dr. Steffy took a handful of the fine soil and packed it inside before standing. "From under the burial stone, you said?"

"Yes, sir."

"This will be intriguing to explore. Why—?"

"Dr. Gist!" A red-haired young woman called from the doorway of the nearby trailer. "We've got the first read-outs for you!"

"Thanks, Kara. I'll be right in."

Dr. Steffy's head tilted. "Read-outs, Stan?" That's not necessary. We've got a direct link to the university computers."

"And I'm linked up at home. But I need more portable information so I can study the data outside when I'm looking after our daughter Maggie," his father explained. Kelsey's been working all hours on her investigative reports, and Maggie's taken to exploring the great Georgia outdoors."

Funny, Tad didn't hear the accusatory tone that he usually did when his father talked about how much better his little sister was doing in adjusting to their new lives.

Maybe the Georgia heat wasn't as bad as he thought, if a person applied the right number sun block. And was in the right person's company. Tad stared at the computer lab trailer's door, willing it to open.

It did. But yet another young woman who wasn't Linda stepped into the doorway to join Kara. "Can you reserve that terminal for me, Anne?" Dr. Steffy asked her.

"If you both step on it!" She called out as an inside voice yelled, "The dust! Close that door!"

Tad was glad the wheelbarrow was almost empty as he lost his father and Dr. Steffy to the project's computers.

What had Dr. Steffy noticed about the soil, Tad wondered as he finished sifting alone. What would it mean to Linda's findings? Had he made a mistake that would be blamed on her?

His task completed, Tad sat beside the pile of sifted dirt and wiped his brow with the back of his arm. He was bone weary. But he also felt more alive than before he'd heard the news of his family's move to Atlanta.

Tad watched the varied members of the dig enter the large tent that was their mess, meeting place and artifact display area. He was impressed by the efficiency of the site, which his dad said was built among the remains of an old Civilian Conservation Corps camp from the 1930s.

A lonesome Foolish Boy trotted over with a low whine. He placed his boney head under Tad's palm for a massage. Tad felt a tap, turned to face a small lady whose head was haloed in gossamer white hair. She put a crockery bowl into his hands. Plunked in its center was a wedge of corn bread.

"Feeding time," she announced in a voice that reminded Tad of Glinda of Oz. "Data entry for the computers, Chick pea stew for us. Boys still have enormous appetites, I hope?"

The savory mix made Tad realize how hungry he was. "I do," he confessed.

The woman smiled like his Aunt Catherine always did when he plunged into one of her enormous family dinners. She set a paper cup of lemonade beside him. Tad missed his Aunt Catherine and her chaotic, welcoming house on Buffalo's East Side.

"I'm Edna Christie."

"Tad Gist."

"Welcome Tad! Play slow pitch softball?"

"I play any kind of ball you've got."

"What position?"

"Shortstop."

"Great. I'll claim you for my side tonight."

"But—"

"It took some convincing. Ball games and stuffy academicians don't always mix. But they're coming along now."

Tad grinned. "You mean you're not a doctor of paleontology, botany, or geology yourself?"

"Me? Lord, no! But I could keep a gaggle of second graders in line as chief cook at Dawson Elementary School! These folks aren't all that different. And some are considerably less polite! Helping out at diggings has been my summer passion for fifty years now. Always enjoyed an explore. So did my Fred. Archeology's like a good ball game, he used to say—anything can happen. Lost him last spring. What a help being at the site has been. And now you're here for Linda. Noticed you when those Cherokee were trying to shake her resolve. You and Foolish Boy were standing by. Our dear girl will be all right now."

"But, Mrs. Christie, I'm not—"

Her strong fluttery hands motioned him closer, as her voice lowered in volume. "Linda needs company besides her spirit woman down there. Most of her people don't approve."

"Do you mean the demonstrators?"

"The Cherokee Coalition, yes. Some say they're armed, not that I've seen any weapons. But these professors are babes in the woods about such things. Fred bought me a gun back in '37 in the C.C.C. days. Times were pretty hardscrabble here then. Well, hard times are back, with the textile mills shutting down.

"Now, Fred and I both fought against the dam coming in too, right up to the state house. But we govern by majority rule, not consensus, like the Cherokee up north do. This isn't their land anymore. They got swindled out of it, sure, but that's the way of it. We're doing what we can to preserve their heritage here, aren't we? How's the stew, Tad?"

"Delicious. And the best corn bread I ever had."

She laughed. "Learned a little about making-do cooking after fifty years, sure! But hunger is the best sauce, especially for you young ones! Some of these studious types, they wolf it down, can't wait to get back to their computers and lab work. Have to coax them onto the softball field. Not living a balanced life, as Linda might say. And that's her mama's corn bread recipe."

"Mrs. Christie, do you think the demonstrators might turn violent?"

"Not unless the local hotheads start a ruckus first, use them as an excuse for generations of bad behavior. A remnant of these locals still believe the Cherokee have hoards of gold hiding in these hills. And, like I say, times are hard. Linda, well, I worry about her. About the ones looking for a scapegoat. Linda's a good target. Dr. Hamilton talks about a scholarship to the university for her next year, imagine, while she's still only sixteen."

Tad swallowed the last of his stew. "Sixteen?"

"Yes."

"She's so... mature."

"And focused. Some might say driven by this project, as hard as it is on her to face Cherokee disapproval."

Tad tried to concentrate on her words, and not on his own delight.

Mrs. Christie noticed. Of course she noticed. Could a kid ever get anything past a school cafeteria lady? Her brow quirked up. "This pleases you, her age?"

Might as well own it. "Yes, ma'am. It makes it easier to think I might, you know, interest her."

She frowned. "Well, what attracts a boy does not work in her favor as site supervisor, young man!"

"Ma'am?"

"They want to take Tallalla away from her, now that the site is yielding such unexpected bounty. 'Too young, can't be trusted,' they say. You'll have to protect her from them too. Are you up to it?" She looked him over hard, then patted his arm. "I'll get you something you'll need."

She turned and whisked away before Tad could tell her that he wasn't staying. Beside him, Foolish Boy whimpered.

"Where are my manners?" Tad apologized, sharing his last mouthful of cornbread with the dog.

When his father flew out the door, Linda wasn't beside him. Tad jumped up, trying to see past him into the trailer's computer center. Linda was intently feeding data into a terminal.

"Finally finished!" Dr. Gist announced. I've got all the read-outs necessary for my weekly report. We can head home. Tad, you've been great about—"

"I don't want to leave, Dad."

"Waiting for Linda? Sure, we can delay a few minutes. But I've got to pick up Maggie at day care, then grab a pizza for dinner and—"

"I mean I don't want to leave at all. I want to join the dig."

"What? Now?"

"They're working against time with that dam coming in, right? They need volunteers. Look, you and Mom have been great since we've been down here. Even Maggie's been putting up with me flying off the handle at her every little annoyance."

Tad looked at the members of the dig site as they exited the mess tent absently eating Mrs. Christie's blondies as they discussed the day's findings. Tad felt even more like the spoiled brat his mother had called him the night before.

"You've all been babysitting me," he told his astonished father now, "showing me the sights, looking for ways to help me adjust. Well, maybe I need something like this, you know, Dad? I was talking to this volunteer, Mrs. Christie. Her husband died last year and she's here, working, instead of feeling sorry for herself. That's what I've been doing since we got down here, feeling sorry for myself. I'd like to try this instead."

"Extraordinary woman, this Mrs. Christie."

"We talked about Linda, too. She's only sixteen. And Dr. Hamilton promised her an assistant but never delivered. I don't think Linda would mind if I helped her. We hit it off pretty well. And you know I haven't been easy to get along with lately."

His father stayed silent as he stroked his chin with a knuckled finger. "Maggie will miss you," he finally said.

"And I'll miss her. And you and Mom. But maybe I need to miss you all for awhile, you know?"

"Careful. You almost said 'y'all.'"

"Not in a million years!"

His father placed his hand on Tad's shoulder. It came straight across now. Their identical six feet height was something Tad was still getting used to since his latest growth spurt.

"I'll talk with Dr. Hamilton," Stan Gist promised, then disappeared into the computer lab trailer again.

Tad watched what was going on through the plexiglass window. Linda rose from her terminal and joined an animated discussion that kept attracting participants. Dr. Steffy got involved, punctuating the air with his pipe.

Tad walked back to Foolish Boy, took up his forgotten cup of lemonade, and finished it off. What had gotten into him, anyway? He wasn't impulsive. He always considered all angles before making any decision about school, sports, even girls. He was a planner. Until the family sprung this move on him. Was he trying to punish them for the quick decision to uproot?

Lost in thought, he caught the scent of sage. Linda rested her hand at his shoulder, startling him.

"I hear you want to join us, Buffalo Man," she said lightly, before her eyes looked more deeply into his. "Oh, Tad. Are you having second thoughts?"

He shrugged, trying to cover his awe at her mind-reading. His mother did that. Kelsey Doyle said he had that kind of face, but she had been sticking microphones in front of people's faces for a dozen years as a news correspondent, so she was practiced. But even Maggie guessed what was on his mind, so maybe his mom was right.

Linda sat beside him on the bench. "Tad, if they decide against you, it might be because of me."

"You don't want my help?"

"Of course I do! And Dr. Hamilton has been trying for a long time to get a graduate student that I took you for, but he doesn't want to overrule Dr. Duncan, who is the administrative director."

Tad smiled. And Dr. Duncan's the choosy type?"

"Not at first. At first he just kept a tight hold on the purse strings of the expedition. But then the mounds started yielding wonderful artifacts. Now he's nervous about me being site supervisor even in my far corner. Dr. Duncan values what we find, and the Mississippian culture of the mound builders. And he's been involved in the project since it began, just as I have. It is hard for me to understand his objections. I've learned much over these summers, he sees that. Still, I feel that maybe Dr. Duncan would like to find someone to supervise me, not for me to supervise."

"And nobody will pretend to know more than you do?"

She looked down at her feet. Tad thought he saw a burgundy color rise to her cheeks before she looked up at him.

"Your father is making a good effort on your behalf. Whichever way it goes, know my thanks."

The door opened. His father emerged and stood before them.

"You've got one week's trial period."

Tad grinned. "Thanks, Dad."

"Use the sun block."

"Okay."

"And you'll need—"

"A hat!" Mrs. Christie appeared before then, a purple canvas bag bumping at her hip. She pulled a worn brown fedora from its depths. Around its brim was a frayed red embroidered band, faded by the sun. Mrs. Christie placed it on Tad's head, where it fit like it was made for him.

"There," she said, "my Fred welcomes you."

Chapter Three

Dr. Hamilton, the expedition's lanky director, finished his report of the day. He turned the meeting over to Dr. Duncan, the administrator responsible for the dig's daily routine. Dr. Duncan was the only one of them wearing a tie, and he held his ever-present clipboard. Which of Linda's Cherokee animal clans would he be from, Tad wondered. The chipmunk? Dr. Duncan adjusted his glasses and sniffed the air like one.

Tad knew that Linda admired the man's expertise and his respect for the culture of the ancient people. But Tad also knew that Dr. Duncan didn't want him here. Dr. Hamilton had done a rare thing in going over the administrator's head to allow him to stay.

Tad had no hope of living up to his standards.

"I remind whomever is leaving the flap open upon leaving the mess tent that those who are still eating do not appreciate the extra ration of flies," the administrator began.

Cue eye roll, Tad thought, and his fellow diggers did not disappoint.

Herb Hudson, a geologist and Dr. Steffy's assistant, raised a finger in the air. "Indeed! Don't let any at Mrs. Christe's repast! Superb dessert tonight, Mrs. Christie!"

"Here! here!" many agreed with stamping feet. Mrs. Christie laughed her twittery Glinda giggle, causing a hearty round of applause.

"If I may return to my list, Mr. Hudson?" Dr. Duncan asked pointedly.

"Oh." Herb stopped mid-clap. "Sure."

"Second. Whoever is defacing the latrine walls will refrain and whitewash."

"Aww, Bonaparte," a voice popped up, "Nobody's taking offense."

Dr. Duncan jabbed his glasses back with his thumb. "Who said that?" he demanded. "Who called me that?"

By the silence that followed, Tad figured the French emperor nickname was not usually heard by Dr. Duncan himself.

He thought about what the administrative director was objecting to: the sprinkling of red-lettered graffiti on the plywood walls of the latrine. Jokes like: Who do archeologists invite to their parties? Anyone they can dig up! and: Where do archeologists like to swim? The Dead Sea. Lame jokes, but fun, not offensive, and accompanied by clever, brightly colored illustrations. Why was it such a big deal?

After some muttering, Max Brock stood. "This week's latrine duty crew offers to whitewash on Friday, Dr. Duncan," he said.

There was a long silence. Tad resolved to volunteer for latrine duty. It might help him get on Dr. Duncan's good side. Besides, Max Brock looked like a decent crew boss, as he took a suspicious-looking red marker from behind his ear and placed it next to other colors lined up in his back pocket. Ah, ha. The artist.

"Agreed," Dr. Duncan finally grunted, taking Max up on his offer. And no more defacing university property." He took a breath. "Now, I shall go over tomorrow's assignments, which I have posted—"

"Doc! Have mercy, we can read them ourselves! We're losing light for the game!" came from the back.

Dr. Hamilton stepped forward. "Duncan, I'm afraid we'll have a mutiny in the ranks if we don't allow our hard-working volunteers a little recreational activity."

The soft-spoken dig director was pulling rank for the second time that day, Tad realized.

Dr. Duncan's mouth tightened into a straight line. He stepped back. "Very well," he said. "It seems I'm the only one cognizant of our deadline. All are dismissed, except for directors, site supervisors, and Tad Gist."

Tad pulled his hand through his hair. Did he look that guilty? It was just a little pencil sketch of a zombie rising from a grave near Max's drawing of the Dead Sea.

Beside him, Linda laughed softly. "Relax," she assured him in an accent faintly like the puppet Count from Sesame Street. "The inner sanctum merely wants to extend its welcome, not carbon-date your pencil."

Tad grinned. "I'm better at ball games than meetings."

"You will be tested by both," she said, pulling out her back pocket art pad and an array of felt tip markers. She began doodling, sending a pretty vine up the side of the page.

Tad wondered if Dr. Duncan ever checked the girl's latrine for graffiti.

"That's easy for you to say, boss."

Linda arched an eyebrow until it disappeared in her dark black bangs, but kept framing her page in green leaves.

When the tent emptied of all but Dr. Hamilton, Dr. Duncan, Dr. La Vetra and the site supervisors, Dr. Hamilton called the meeting to order.

Introductions were made. The other site supervisors ranged in age from early twenties graduate students to environmentalist Erla Wingdale, who Tad judged to be in her sixties.

"Besides extending a warm welcome to Tad here," Dr. Hamilton began, "let's congratulate Linda on graduating to full site supervisor, now that she has someone to supervise. Now, let's get to business so we can play ball."

"Great," Rose La Vetra agreed. "We're running low on butterfly bandages and sunblock, Dr. Duncan," she reported.

The administrative director nodded gravely, and put a notation in his book.

"Everyone's in good health, and that's it from me," she concluded.

Dr. Duncan's head rose. "I wish I could say the same for our spirits since our visitors returned."

Linda's doodling stopped in the middle of a red cardinal she was placing among her foliage.

"It's a subject I'd like to discuss, so that our new member behaves appropriately towards the demonstrators," Dr. Duncan continued.

"I have explained to Tad about the purpose of the Cherokee Coalition, Linda offered quietly.

"And about the dam coming in," Tad offered, "and the Peterson Company's plans." He could hear the crack of a bat outside the tent. "Is Mr. Peterson related to the guy who owns the tobacco company?"

"He is 'the guy.' as you say," Dr, Duncan informed him.

"But I thought he was the developer."

"Peterson's involvement is new, Tad," Dr. Steffy took up the conversation. "It's his 'give back' to the community, as he says.

Like Andrew Carnegie's libraries, the Rockefeller art museums. Peterson wants a slew of public recreational areas with his name on them."

"But he does not like it when people of the community object to his plans," Linda said evenly.

"Not 'people.' young woman," Dr. Duncan said. "Only the Cherokee. We should be grateful to Mr. Peterson."

Erla Wingdale spoke up. "Exactly what he's trying to buy. Our gratitude. His angel halo, while he's marketing cigarettes to children and the Third World!"

"Now, Erla," Dr. Hamilton tried to cool the growing debate. "We're not here to—"

But Michael Steffy interrupted. "Linda's right. Peterson will donate his millions his way, or he'll take his marbles and go home. Anyone who objects is being ungrateful. I think the Cherokee have a right to their anger."

Dr. Hamilton raised his hands. "Now, now. Nobody's trying to restrict anyone's right to anger. This is the last effort by the Cherokee to register their dissatisfaction before the dam building starts. Only Linda's been addressed directly, and from what I hear, she handled herself with wisdom beyond her years. What I want to know: is anyone troubled by the presence of the demonstrators?"

"Troubled?" Dr. Duncan spoke up. "Of course we're troubled! Who knows what those Indians have in mind?" His voice rose to a shout. "They think we're in league with Peterson!"

"Are we?" Michael Steffy asked pointedly.

The silence stayed until Mrs. Christie poked her baseball-capped head through the tent flap. "Linda, why don't you invite the Cherokee folks to dinner tomorrow night to talk this out? Who knows? We may get a few more volunteers like Tad here in the bargain?"

Dr. Hamilton smiled. "What an excellent suggestion. "Linda?"

"I'll ask," she agreed. "And I'll make my mother's cornbread."

Tension eased. "Final question," the dig director said. "Are the demonstrators impeding anyone's work?"

Each of the supervisors answered in the negative.

"Then I suggest we go on, happy that our Native American friends are peaceful and persistent in exercising their right of free speech."

"Now get your ornery hides out of here and play ball," Mrs. Christie closed out the meeting for him.

Chapter Four

On the softball field, the hierarchy of the dig site turned upside down. Pete Lowery and Anne Kane, two graduate school assistants opened a canvas bag full of bases, hats, bats, soft balls and gloves. They were in charge and chose players as they handed out team assignments. Tad took his place on Pete's team while Linda was on Anne's side.

Only Dr. Duncan refused invitations to join in. "Someone has to make up a list of work assignments for tomorrow," he groused, tucking his clipboard under his arm and heading for the computer lab trailer.

Once on the field, everyone's name changed. Geologist Michael Steffy put his pipe away, rolled up his checkered sleeves, flexed his arm muscles and became "Stonewall." It was difficult for anyone to get a ball past him, and he hit well, too.

"Medicine Woman" (Dr. LaVetra) specialized in neat bunts to third base, her blond pony tail flying.

"Planter" was botanist Max Brock. The swirling vine-like signals he gave as catcher baffled the opposing team. And sometimes, his own pitcher.

"Steel Man" was derived from both photographer Bill Steele's name and the dashing silver streak that ran through his hair. To top it off, he used a metal bat to sail his hits to right field.

Linda was "Little Mound Woman" to honor her dig site. She had already dubbed Tad "Buffalo Man," and the name stuck here on the field of play.

The atmosphere of this world after work reminded Tad of a multi-generational scout camp. The mood was festive and good-natured, a contrast to the serious and sometimes confrontational meeting.

For the next five blissful innings, Tad felt at last connected to the Georgia soil as he helped Pete's "Trench Eagles" to a six to four lead over Anne's "Dusters."

As shortstop, Tad managed to block almost every ball hit his way. But after driving two runners home with a double to right field, Linda next put him out neatly when he tried to steal third base. He groused that he was a baseball player, not used to softball's short fielder behind the second baseman, but admitted it was Linda's accurate throw that retired his side.

Then Pete Lowery's pitching arm tired, losing out to Linda's strong-armed connection with his curve ball. Her single drove the winning run home in the last inning. Tad didn't mind losing, especially to Linda's hard drive.

"Good game," he told her, and meant it, as his team congratulated the winners.

"I like the way you play it, Buffalo Man," she said softly.

Their cheers sent Dr. Duncan out from his self-imposed exile, his clipboard full of the next day's assignments. That task complete, he went on to a list of more regulations. Tad found himself giving in to a pleasant drowsiness that the day's work, a good meal, and the game produced. It didn't help that he and Linda had crashed down on the ground in a semicircle of star-gazers, and that his head was comfortably resting in Foolish Boy's fur.

The rhythmic beating of the dog's heart kept pace with something...what was it? A dream. Of watching his own feet, and the dog's running, running. Where? Through the Georgia night, ink back. Where were they? He had to find Linda. Where was she? At her Little Mound, digging under Tallalla's grave stone. He tried to adjust his eyes to all the darkness. He couldn't see her. He tried calling, but his voice wouldn't work. He had to go down, to get her out, before she was buried, because the ground was shaking, cracking open.

He sat up with a start. Mrs. Christie's hand was at his shoulder. "Easy, dear," she crooned.

"What was that?"

"A crack of thunder. An empty threat of rain, I suspect, as my corns are not acting up."

Tad shook his head and looked around.

Foolish Boy whined softly, still beneath him. He sat up. Linda's light denim jacket fell from his shoulders. But she was gone. Everybody was gone except the gossamer-haired lady. She clucked sympathetically.

"Bad dream?"

"Yes."

"That comes from being in a strange place. Come. We have a cot set up in the men's tent for our master shortstop."

Tad groaned, rubbing his stiff neck. "What time is it?"

"Past midnight."

"Last I remember was…I guess I haven't endeared myself to Dr. Duncan, have I?"

"Oh, none of us has managed that," Mrs. Christie assured him.

Mrs. Christie's soft grey curls exploded out from an Atlanta baseball cap so old it might have qualified as an artifact itself.

Tad grinned, remembering their game. "That was some slide." he complimented her.

"Now that you showed me your technique, I'll never get tagged out by one of those data punching academics again!" she proclaimed.

Foolish Boy finally rose to his feet.

"Come on, you two, I'll show you the way," Mrs. Christie offered.

Tad stood. She slipped her arm through his and leaned into his side. "Just tell me the jokes on the men's latrine walls before I tuck you in, won't you, dear?" she asked.

Chapter Five

It was still dark. A dry tongue licked Tad's cheek. It felt much better than the clanging inside his head from the sound of the wind-up alarm clock next to Dr. Duncan's cot. Tad opened one eye. Did its hands really point to four o'clock? Even more grating was its owner's voice.

"Who left that flap open?" he demanded.

"I must have, sir," Tad admitted. "Sorry."

"Not an exemplary start, young man. One spider bite that swells your face to the size of one of your softballs will be enough to remind you."

"Ease up on the kid, Duncan," Bill Steele's gravely voice came from the tent's corner. "I came in last, not him."

"Poker game," Dr. Duncan guessed.

"A friendly, relaxing diversion," the photographer insisted. "Promotes comradeship between ourselves and the locals. You ought to try it some time. And Mike made out pretty well for himself, didn't you—Hey, Carlos, where's Mike Steffy?"

"I don't know," came the mumbled reply.

The project's photographer reached for his pants. "Mrs. Christie must be making western omelettes this morning. Mike beats everybody to the mess tent for those."

Dr. Duncan stood over Tad. "That dog has been at your feet all night."

"And?"

"The women may tolerate that animal, but I have allergies. Leave him outside tonight. He'll find his way to their tent."

"Okay, sure."

Dr. Duncan stomped off past him. Tad caught sight of red silk boxer shorts as a breeze picked up the side of his robe. A pillow hit the tent flap just behind him.

Linda was leaning over a steaming cup when Foolish Boy left Tad's side and trotted up to her.

"There you are!" she welcomed him with a deep rub behind his ears. "Did you feel the need to protect my new assistant all night?"

Tad frowned, remembering his dream. "Did I miss much, slugger?" he asked, trying to change the subject.

"Only a lot of laughing in the women's tent, once Mrs. Christie told us the jokes you put on the men's latrine walls,"

"Me?"

"'What did one archeologist say to another? I've got a bone to pick with you?' Lame, Tad!"

"I only told her the jokes! I didn't write them!"

"So our mysterious defacer of university property has yet to show himself?"

"Or herself."

"Tad, the ah... witticisms are in the men's latrine."

"A place you women are very curious about," he teased, dropping her denim jack over her shoulders. "Thanks for tucking me in. And for the pillow," he added, rubbing Foolish Boy's knobby head.

Linda buried her face in the jacket's sleeve and inhaled deeply. "Hmmm...Sun block, blondie crumbs, and damp Foolish Boy," she purred.

Tad grunted. Although he'd "washed out a few things" as his mother would delicately put rinsing and hanging his underwear overnight, he felt as fresh as leftover bacon. And Linda, from her heavy work boots to the new blue kerchief that replaced yesterday's red one, looked, well, terrific.

"Is that high test coffee?" he growled.

"High test? Oh, caffeinated, you mean? It's chicory root. No test, I'm afraid. But very good. Try it?" She offered a taste.

Just seeing a smear of her honey-scented lip gloss on the cup's rim woke him up further. "Maybe tomorrow. Today I need octane. How did those old guys stay up playing poker?"

Linda smiled. "They weren't showing magnificent softball skills earlier."

"Or knocking hits through my defense line," he reminded her.

"The poker game is a twice-a-week ritual in town with some local men. They even invite Dr. LaVetra. Maybe they'll invite you, when you manage to stay awake longer," she added with a sly grin.

"Aw, I wouldn't be of any use."

"Why?"

"My face is the map of my mind, heart and soul, my mother tells me. I should never play poker."

Linda laughed. "She may be right, Buffalo Man! But there are other attractions in town—dancing, Square, line, and even 1940s swing. And a show."

"Show?"

"Movie house. With two screens!"

"And here I was thinking I was in the wilderness."

"Huh. City men are hard to please."

"Only this early in the morning." Tad tried to redeem himself in her eyes.

She stood and took his hand. "Come on, I'll show you how to get your coffee and some breakfast."

She walked him through the breakfast line. Mrs. Christie piled his plate high with poached eggs, home fries and bacon. They returned to their table where Tad downed his coffee and nibbled at his toast while Linda began demolishing every morsel on her plate. Where did she put it all?

"Hollow leg?" he asked her.

"Not a morning person?" she fired back.

"It's still dark. Not morning."

Pre-dawn, maybe. But morning."

"Maybe if the eggs didn't look like they're staring at me."

"Listen, Buffalo Man," Linda said, forking a triangle of egg into her mouth, "the sun will be baking by ten o'clock, frying us by noon. Dinner's not until one. Mrs. Christie will send us off with a snack and water, but that's a long eight hours in the field. I intend to get a full day's work out of you. Eat."

She pointed her chin to the angelic woman in the flowered apron. "And it won't do to insult the cook."

Tad groaned but managed to eat one of his eggs. The other he slipped to a grateful Foolish Boy.

At least the strong black coffee was taking effect as Linda led Tad to the artifact tables.

Carlos Mazza, a big guy who threw a good, accurate pitch, touched Linda's elbow. "Have you seen Dr. Steffy? He asked me to test some soil samples, but I can't find him."

Tad remembered his talk with Dr. Steffy. Was it the soil from Linda's site?

"Try in the computer lab," Dr. Duncan called from two tables over.

"Or maybe he's calling his stock broker to invest his big winnings from last night," Bill Steele offered, earning a disapproving look from the university administrator. Dr. Steffy's assistant thanked them and moved on.

At the artifact table Tad saw proof of Linda's great work. Tallalla's pipe stems had an honored place among stone axes, bowls and pots that showed both ingenuity and beauty. Carved mica, animal teeth and shells demonstrated a far-ranging trading network as well as artistic skill.

Tad followed the etched out sunbursts, crosses, and human eyes, as well as abstract designs. He got lost in them until he heard a whispered call. He raised his head to see a wooden mask with horrible, twisted openings for eyes, nose and mouth. Linda peeked out from behind it.

"We found several of these the first year of the dig. They were buried in a circle around the site."

"What are they?"

"Booger masks. We use them in one of our dances, even today. A funny dance, to scare away strangers."

"Like me."

"Well, yes." She placed the mask against his face. "In the dance we would sit you down and make demands. 'Who are you?' and 'What is your name?' and 'Where do you come from?'"

"And what do I answer, the truth?"

"Oh, no. You say silly things, like your latrine jokes."

"They're not my jokes!"

Tad took the mask from his face and stared at its exaggerated features. "Why were they buried around the site?"

"We don't know. It is not like the Principal People to disturb the ancient's burial sites. The masks are from later, from contact time."

"Contact time?"

"Contact with the Europeans. For the Cherokee it came first with the Spanish in 1540. Maybe the mask people were trying to keep the mound builders safe from the strangers."

"What about now? Hey, you're the only one the mound builders welcome here. I'm glad I'm your assistant!"

Linda's looked thoughtful, not amused. "Maybe," she said, reaching for the mask.

He held on to it. "Did I say something wrong?"

"No."

"Sure I did. Listen, Linda. I'm not always a jerk. This thing scares me. I'm trying to chase away my own fear."

"You, courageous Taddeusz?" she asked softly.

"Sure. I know I'm the stranger here. I have to prove myself to all of you. And to myself. But yesterday, walking back from the site with you...well, that's the first time since I moved down here that I felt I might belong."

61

"Even though you were with me? Another stranger?"

"You, a stranger?"

"Of course. Everyone else is—"

"But you're also among your relatives. In your own country."

"This country has not been ours for a long time, Buffalo Man."

Tad released the mask into her hands.

They walked together to get their buckets and wheelbarrow. Foolish Boy came too, but bounding ahead, so Tad was close enough to feel Linda's heat and catch the scent of her…fresh and green. Not at all like the heavy flowery perfume that Julie Tolliver's good-bye letter was doused in. He'd written Julie three letters since then, with no answer. He guessed it really was good-bye, despite all the lacy hearts she'd drawn on the pages.

Did Linda have a boyfriend? What was a not-stupid way to ask her? The closest Tad had come to a girl lately was rescuing damsels in distress by destroying the evil trolls of his computer games or watching moms win TV game shows.

As impulsive as his decision was to join the dig, maybe it was the right one.

But the closer they got to Little Mound, the more Tad dreaded climbing down that ladder into the ancient artisan's grave. Especially before the sun was up. And yesterday he was visiting. Today it was his job. He had to get over it.

Linda shone her flashlight around the perimeter of the tarp as Tad found the ladder. When he returned with it, she was still scanning. Foolish Boy sniffed around the tarp's edges.

"Something is wrong," Linda whispered.

Tad put the ladder down. "What?"

"The stones."

"Stones?"

"The ones we used to anchor the tarp, Tad. They are spaced too far apart."

"Maybe the wind—"

"It was still, except for the thunder."

Foolish Boy let out a low whine, and circled the site slowly. Tad ran his hand through his hair. Linda rubbed the arms of her denim jacket, as if she was cold. Tad touched her back. "Maybe an animal tried to get in?"

"Yes, maybe," she said, then shrugged. "You'd think I'd be used to this after three summers."

"Used to what?"

She made a gesture encircling Little Mound, then wider, around the other gashes in the earth. "I have asked Tallalla's forgiveness. I have burned cedar here. I sing to her. And I have promised to burn tobacco, to reconsecrate this place before it is flooded. Is that enough?"

She stared at the tarp. "Dr. Hamilton has promised me that she will not be moved from here. But I don't know if it is right. If I am doing things in the right way. I don't know, Tad."

This was not the sure, confident Linda he's met yesterday, Tad realized. This was not the laughing Linda. "Let's ask her together," he said quietly.

She looked up at him. "It may be she has answered already. By sending you."

"Yeah? Like, to protect you?"

She frowned. "I can protect myself, shortstop."

He held up his hands. "Okay, I deserved that."

Linda's smile returned as they removed the anchoring stones together and folded back the tarp.

When they lowered the ladder, Foolish Boy was still restlessly circling the pit.

"*Hi hwi lo hi!*" Linda instructed impatiently as she stood on the top rung.

Foolish Boy whimpered, then yelped twice.

"No, *kwa!*" she said, waving her arm toward the folded tarp.

The dog retreated but did not lay down. He stood, alert and panting.

Tad smiled. "I guess we're all a little nervous today," he said.

Linda shone the flashlight downward as she descended into the pit. Tad watched her blue headscarf disappear in the darkness before he switched his own flashlight on and directed it toward her voice.

"Made it," she assured him. "I'll steady the ladder so you can bring down the—wait. How strange."

"What?" Tad called down. "Linda, what's strange?"

He heard a rumbling noise, then a soft cry. He couldn't see her.

"Linda!" Tad swung his leg around the ladder.

"It's all right. I just slipped."

"I'm coming," he told her. "Don't move. I'm coming down."

The ladder tilted as it took on his greater weight, then settled more firmly in the soil.

"Slipped?" he asked as he descended. "Slipped on what?"

"Oh. Oh, no." Her voice was a soft, forsaken whisper. It froze his blood.

Tad looked down over his shoulder in time to see Linda reaching for the skull on the stone brier. Out of its eye socket a broad head appeared, flicking a two-pronged tongue.

The snake spilled out of the skull further. There seemed no end to it. Diamond-shaped blotches edged in yellow covered its body. It moved from side to side, tracing around Linda's outstretched hand.

She retreated slowly, silently. There, within Tad's grasp. He reached his arm down to her waist and anchored a finger in the belt loop of her jeans. The snake opened its mouth. Wide. The hollow fangs in its upper jaw appeared.

Tad pulled with all his might.

The snake struck once. Again. It was only then that Linda screamed.

Chapter Six

Linda's blunt, clipped nails dug deeper into his back.

"Almost there," he breathed into her blue kerchief.

She nodded there, under his heart.

The ladder slipped, threatening to send them both back down to the digging floor. Tad caught a fleeting glimpse of a shadow under the concave burial rock, with a dark stain emanating from it. That must have been where Linda had stumbled.

He kept climbing. One step, another. Above them a rose-colored light lit the eastern horizon.

Tad's head cleared the surface. In the distance, Foolish Boy was barking as if there was a bear at his heels. A bear of a man in blue overalls was.

He got down on his hands and knees and grabbed Tad under his arms. He pulled, and both Tad and Linda soon collapsed on the surface of Little Mound like a couple of rag dolls.

Gently, Tad rolled Linda over.

The big, full-bearded guy who'd pulled them out stood above them. "Where?" he asked.

Linda raised herself to her elbows. "My foot," she told him quietly. Her leg shook. "My left foot."

The man lifted her heavy work boot, which was like a child's in his grip. "Hold her leg steady, boy," he instructed Tad gruffly.

Tad gripped above where Linda's heavy work socks ended. Her breathing was even. Foolish Boy howled. Embedded in the metal-ringed shoelace hole was the snake's fang, dripping venom.

The big man plucked it out, held it up.

Tad slipped the boot from Linda's foot. He pulled off her sock and examined her skin. It was unbroken.

"Where else?" Tad asked, raising his voice over Foolish Boy's whine. "Linda, where else are you hurt?"

"I am not hurt," she answered in that same, flat, calm voice.

Tad's fingers began to shake. "But you're bleeding."

She looked down at her splattered clothes. "It is not my blood."

The big man standing over them gently placed the fang into the small pocket in the bib of his overalls. "Whose is it, missy?"

"Dr. Steffy's. He's under the burial stone. He's dead."

The man blinked. "Are you sure?"

"Yes."

"Not by my Moses!"

"No. I tried to help, but—so much blood."

Tad felt punched in the gut.

Foolish Boy nudged his head under Linda's arm, whining louder.

"I should have gone down first," Tad said.

No." Linda pointed to the low dock siders that were fine for sitting out on his porch in Inman Park, but hardly here.

He reached for the big man's arm as he turned toward the dig opening.

"There's a snake—" he warned.

The man nodded. "I know that, boy. Moses is an Eastern Diamondback rattler. *Crotalus adamanteus,*" if we're being formal."

"I didn't hear a rattle," Tad said, from a voice suddenly gone dry.

"They don't always rattle, like in the movies. Linda, would you hush up that mutt of yours, so I can hear myself think?"

"*Wa to, wa to,*" Linda urged Foolish Boy, a weariness cutting through the flat tone of her voice.

His whine finally silenced when she rubbed the flabby skin around his neck. "And *wa to,* Mr. Barker."

"Don't be casting your spells on me, missy," the giant man warned.

"I said 'thank you,' sir. For listening to Foolish Boy. For coming to help us."

"I only just hauled. It's the boy got you out. If you weren't scratching the shirt off his back, you'd have seen that."

Tad watched a little color flash in her cheeks. She pulled up his shirt. "Welts. I did. I scratched you."

"It's nothing. Linda—"

"How do you know? You can't see it! Tad can't see it, can he, Mr. Barker?"

The big man grunted, concern in his eyes. "Linda Tassel, listen to me. You should leave this troubled dig site for the men to fight over. Take me up on my offer. Come over and be the Gold Mine Indian Princess in my show."

She breathed out a small sigh. "You know the Cherokee have no princesses, Mr. Barker."

"Daughter of a chief, then?"

"The *Tsa la ki"* are children of our mothers."

He snorted, reaching his hand to Tad's shoulder. They were doing this together, he and the giant man, Tad realized. They were working to bring Linda back from her strange, trancelike state with teasing, distracting her from all she'd seen below.

"Caleb Barker of El Dorado Diggings just up river," he introduced himself. "Tad, is it?"

"Yes, sir. Tad Gist."

"Been trying to get Linda here to be the star attraction of my summer show for the

70

tourists. Could earn enough to put herself through that fancy Atlanta university! She can call herself whatever she'd like. She can sing, dance, sell her trinkets…even make it educational." He turned to Linda now. "How about it, little lady? When are you going to trade dirt for your own throne at my show?"

Linda giggled softly, shaking her head. Then she laughed. Too hard, Tad thought. Tears were forming at the rims of her eyes, then spilled down her face.

Tad looked helplessly at Caleb Barker, at Foolish Boy. Both nodded. He took Linda's shaking arms and pulled gently. He needed to hold her. She pressed herself against his chest. Tad stroked the hair that spilled out of her kerchief while the big man patted her shoulder.

"There, now," he approved, "hold on while I get my Moses out of there.

"Take her back to their base camp, son," he advised, "to that lady doctor. Tell Hamilton to call in the sheriff. Linda doesn't have to see anything else. We'll let the police handle things now."

Tad watched the big man retrieve a long-handled hook from a canvas sack. Linda lifted her head. She and Tad watched as Mr. Barker circled Little Mound with surprising agility. He poked and prodded within the hole.

"Got you!" he proclaimed, holding up the noosed snake. Moses struck out ineffectively. The diamondback's mouth was wide open, it's one remaining fang erect. Tad shivered, despite the rising heat of the day as the snake's rattles pounded against the big man's shins.

"Will Moses be all right, Mr. Barker?" Linda asked.

"Sure, little lady."

"And he'll grow a new fang?"

"As deadly as the last."

"That's good."

Tad wondered at her concern for a creature that almost inflicted a deadly bite. "You're being awfully generous about that brute."

"No, she's not," Caleb Barker informed him. "She's just being Cherokee. Rattlers are supernaturals, intimate with the rain and thunder gods. Bad luck to cross them."

Linda shook her head. "You know that, and not about Indian princesses, Mr. Barker?"

"That's snake lore. I know everything about snakes."

Linda groaned. Tad enjoyed the rhythm of the teasing war and the healing effect it seemed to be having on Linda. He took her hand as they rose to their feet and turned toward base camp.

"New exhibit! How about: 'Cave of the One-Fanged Diamondback!' How does that sound?" Caleb Barker shouted after them. "Maybe I'll build Moses a royal throne to make you envious, Linda Tassel! Then you'll come and work for me at El Dorado. I know women!"

"Not this one, Mr. Barker!" she sang back at him, her voice and walk stronger.

Chapter Seven

The man before them had a close shaven head, and a prickly silver growth of beard. About sixty, Tad guessed, with laugh lines etched around his eyes so deeply that he seemed amused by everything. That didn't match his profession, and all the grizzly sights he must have seen over his years as chief of the criminal investigative division of the Atlanta police department.

He also looked like what he was, a trout fisherman hauled off Lake Lanier, from his chino pants, to the feathery flies in his pork-pie hat.

As he sat across the table from the man, Tad took the dog-eared business card from his hand. The metro Atlanta number was scratched out and another penciled in.

He looked up at W. C. Hawes as the man spoke. "'What's the W. C. stand for?' right?"

"Sir?"

"That's what all you Yankees want to know. Not used to our ways. Well, down in Atlanta, I tell them they stand for 'We Convict.' Made me a living legend. Retired ten years ago. I'm only part-time division chief with the department in Cartersville now. Don't have much need for a calling card around here. Well, they reeled me in on this case because not a mother's son of them's investigated a murder before. You all right, son?"

"Me? Sure. I didn't see what Linda did, sir." Tad looked toward the shadows inside the medical tent.

"Don't you worry," he advised, his tone softening a notch. "She did real well, remembering what she could before you yanked her out of there." He shook his head. "Awful thing for her to see. Looks like a ritual killing."

"Ritual?"

"No heart. Then that carnival show rattler goes for her besides. Did you know Dr. Steffy well, Tad?"

"No. I only joined the dig yesterday."

"That's right, new kid in town. Your father is the new coordinating anthropologist at the university down in Atlanta?"

"That's right, sir."

How many people had Hawes already talked with, Tad wondered. His hands held no notebook, no clipboard. He was the opposite of Dr. Duncan in that way. But with or without notes, Tad didn't imagine much got past W. C. Hawes.

"Well," he drawled out now, "Sometimes an outsider's perspective is the best of all.

Tell me, Tad. How did Dr. Steffy seem to get along with the rest of the folks here?"

"Very well, sir."

"No problems you could see with his peers, or with the folks working under him?"

"It's hard for me to tell who's in charge and who's working under them, except for Dr. Hamilton and Dr. Duncan."

"The main overseers?"

Tad winced. This wasn't a plantation. "I guess you could say so, sir."

"But you wouldn't."

"Linda calls Dr. Hamilton Dig Boss, Detective."

"And that sits with your Yankee sensibilities better?"

A long, steady look from eyes that demanded an answer, not a shrug of teen-aged mumble. The laugh lines remained, of course, belying the suddenly charged air between them.

"Yes, sir," Tad said evenly.

That got him a genuine smile before W.C. Hawes scratched his chin whiskers. "You had any contact with Dr. Steffy yesterday?"

"Yes. When he looked over the dirt my dad and I were sifting through at the end of the day. He said I was a good observer," Tad remembered with a sting of pain at the loss of a man he'd barely met. "I only watched from outside the trailer when they discussed my joining the dig site, but I think he was pulling for me."

"How do you reckon that?"

"The way he gestured with his pipe," Tad admitted sheepishly.

"Maybe you're not so glad he helped get you the job now?"

"Oh, no! I'd hate to think of Linda being alone this morning."

The detective grunted softly. "It sounds to me like clinical shock that little girl was going into before you and that huckster Caleb Barker drew her out."

"Is that right, sir? Shock?"

"That's what the doctor says."

"Linda seems okay to you now, doesn't she, Chief Hawes?"

"Yep. Wants to get back to her trench with her remains of that even smaller artist lady, too. I can't figure why. But the doc thinks it's good to get things as close to normal and routine as possible, once our team is gone. Body's been rushed out so we can take liver temperature, establish time of death. The outdoors is not the best place for a murder, from our point of view."

"How's that, sir?"

"Impression prints easily destroyed. Remains touched by animals, insects. Amongst us, the nature of the murder, and that snake, I'm afraid you two will have your restoration work cut out for you, once we open up the site to you again. You will stay and stand by that little girl, won't you, son?"

"That little girl is my boss, Chief Hawes. Sure I'll stand by her."

"Well, don't get your Yankee self all cattywumpus, boy. That's good. That's good to hear. Some don't see you as the steady type around here. But not all. 'Course, if I were Linda's daddy, I'd be asking you about the nature of your intentions."

The compact man took his hat between his hands and stroked a bright green fly feather with his thumb. "Any other contact with Dr. Steffy?"

"We all played a softball game last night," Tad remembered. "Except for Dr. Duncan."

"Where was he?"

"In with the computers."

"Why?"

"Planning out things for today's work, I think."

"And he came out with the assignments, I'm told. He gave them out to everyone, without any disputes?"

"I guess. Fact is, Linda and I, there on the field after the game? We were star-gazing and I sort of fell asleep."

"In the company of that little—in your boss's company?"

"Well. yeah."

"Maybe her daddy's got nothing to worry about after all. How did Dr. Steffy play ball, son?"

Tad thought. "I caught two of his drives, but one he got by me."

"Single?"

"Double."

"He could run, then?"

"Yeah," Tad remembered. "Quick on his feet. Did Dr. Steffy try to run from his killer, sir?"

"Hard to tell. Botched job. Awfully messy ritual, if it was. With a dull knife, too. But that came after."

Tad forced the wad of bile back down his throat. "After?"

"Shotgun, close range, through the heart and lungs both. Maybe already dead when he was knifed open. Like it was a second thought. Or a cover-up."

"Chief Hawes, you don't think—"

"No, I do not. I scrupulously avoid thinking at this stage of the game. Now's the time I gather, see? It's a long trail. From identifying the criminal, to apprehending, to proving guilt in a court of law. I need motive, opportunity, and evidence before I can even begin to nail whoever killed Michael Steffy, a fellow who studied rocks and dirt and could run bases and make steadfast friends and at least one powerful enemy. Let's hope it was not a whole nation of enemies."

"The Cherokee," Tad whispered.

"I'll tell you something, son. That little girl could have been paralyzed or dead from a snakebite now, her liver in the medical examiner's hands. We've been keeping an eye on the Cherokee visitors—the ones down off their reservations in North Carolina ever since the dam was a rumor. Can't say much for their organizational skills, and they sure run on Indian time. Those two things make it hard to establish patterns. Damn inconvenient people to investigate, which I'm sure pleases them no end. And no arrests. Not so much as a barroom brawl in the three years they've been crossing state lines. Which might, of course, spell the discipline of fanatics."

"But you don't think so?"

"Remember what I said about thinking?" The chief stood. "Well, I've got a long day ahead." He looked past Tad and his voice went gravely with anger. "And it's not going to be made any easier by way of that blamed woman. She and her own viper squad are here so fast I have half a mind to consider them suspects."

Tad turned, seeing the woman in question, flanked by her cameramen, struggling over the incline in her high heels and peach linen suit.

Tad smiled. "Hi, Mom," he said.

Chapter Eight

The sound man dropped a duffle bag at Tad's feet. "Here you go, Indiana Jones," he said. "Clothes for your adventure."

"Thanks," Tad said, wishing the bag didn't have a designer label. His mother introduced herself and her producer to a grim-faced Chief Hawes.

She turned. "An establishing shot of the mounds from the river, please, guys?" she asked.

"Watch out for snakes," Chief Hawes barked. "And keep behind crime scene barriers or you'll be flying back to Atlanta without a plane!"

The two men froze in their tracks. Kelsey Doyle shook her head. Tad noticed the nervous twitch around her mouth. She laughed, which is what she always did to hide it. "They are fish out of water once we're beyond the I-285. They'd rather cover a riot than be out in this glorious countryside."

"Not so glorious today, Miss Doyle," Chief Hawes reminded her, fingering the crisp business card she'd presented him, along with a look at her press credentials. "Now, before you all scatter, would you mind telling me by what means your news organization got wind of our unfortunate event so soon?"

Sidney Perdue, the Current News producer that was her least favorite working partner, adjusted his striped vest. "Vigilant monitoring of your radio communications with mobile units while we were on our way up from Atlanta, sir," he claimed.

Tad watched his mom step in between the two men. "Let's start at the beginning, Sidney," she said. "I was assigned to do a feature story on the digging, Chief Hawes," she explained. "With Morris University's permission to shoot footage, of course."

W.C. Hawes tilted his head. "That blowhard Brett Lowman sent you up here for a feature story?"

His mom drew herself up as best she could with her heels sinking in the loose soil. "A series of reports, actually. There are many aspects to this story. And frankly, now there's one more."

"Wonderful. Throw a little more gasoline on this fire."

Sidney Perdue's mustache twitched, but his mother silenced him with a look. "We didn't create it, sir," she said quietly. "We're reporting."

"See that you and your team do so responsibly," Miss Doyle."

She nodded and sent her scowling producer to catch up with the camera crew. Then she smudged Tad's clay-smudged brow with her finger. "Right now, Chief Hawes, I'd like to assure myself of my son's well-being. Are you finished with him?"

He nodded towards Tad. "Hardly, as he and Miss Tassel found the body. But I will not come between a concerned mother and her son at this time."

W.C. Hawes retreated, consulting with a policeman.

Tad's mother squeezed his hand. "Your father and I thought this was such a good idea last night. What an awful thing! I drove your car up. You can come home with—"

"No, Mom, please. Dr. Steffy fought hard for me to stay. I'd feel I was letting him down if I left now."

Kelsey sighed. "Yes. That's why your father insisted I bring up your bag. Open it. Maggie's drawings are on top."

Tad feasted on his little sister's images of the family holding hands. One was in the snows of Buffalo, the other in the smiling sun of Atlanta. In each, her fanciful dragons and flying cats hovered over them like angels. Tad found himself missing Maggie with an ache in his heart.

Under the drawings was an array of designer work clothes, new hiking boots, and packaged gourmet snacks and sweets, with a three-pound smoked Polish kielbasa at the bottom. Tad held it up in triumph, surprised by his own delight.

"Mom, where did you find this?"

"Foods of the World in Buckhead. Paid three times what Mr. Kazarski charged us on East Seventh Street! I guess kielbasa's a delicacy here, along with the raspberry truffles and stuffed artichoke hearts."

"It's all great, Mom, thanks," Tad said, though he wished she'd just brought his old clothes.

"Put on the boots right away, will you, Tad?"

"Do," Linda urged as she joined them. She looked better, much better than when Dr. Rose made her sit on a cot in the medical tent's cool corner for her first round of police questioning.

Tad took her hand. "Mom, I'd like you to meet Linda Tassel."

Everyone's schedule was disrupted at the dig, between the police work and the time Kelsey Doyle's interviews took.

His mom treated Linda like the professional she was as Linda pointed out artifacts in the main tent.

"I understand the Cherokee people are divided in regard to the work being done here."

Linda considered carefully. "I believe most of us are unhappy that the dam will put the old ones underwater," she explained.

"We don't separate sacred from secular spaces. We believe the spirit world intermingles with the physical world."

"Why aren't more Cherokee here, helping preserve their heritage?"

"You would have to ask them."

"You have?"

"Yes."

"Will you tell me what you've learned?"

Linda frowned. She was finding out how hard it was to evade Kelsey Doyle's persistent questioning. "For some, I think the problem is a general distrust, the reasons based in politics, money, power, racism. Some of the Cherokee fear the university dig does not observe proper rituals, I think. That would give the space negative power."

Kelsey nodded. "But you are part of the dig, and also a member of the Cherokee nation. Are your concerns honored by the university?"

"Oh, yes." Linda' eyes shone. Tad wondered if the camera was capturing it.

"Might you tell us what rituals you've observed at your dig site to honor the traditions of your people? Kelsey probed further.

Linda smiled warmly at Tad, standing beside the cameraman. Viewers would think the smile was for them, Tad knew from watching his mother at work since he was a small boy. He wasn't sure how he felt about sharing Linda's smile with the Atlanta television audience. She reached for a cedar bough, and explained the nature and beauty of Tallalla's work as a pipe stem carver, and how she sought to reconsecrate her remains when the dig's mission was complete.

Later the camera crew, ordered about by Sidney Perdue, worked in the reporting on the police investigation. Kelsey Doyle informed Dr. Hamilton that a piece to promote the later aired documentary as well as the news piece about the murder would be prepared for tonight's broadcast.

Chapter Nine

Through the afternoon Little Mound was ringed by yellow plastic, warning people away from the crime scene. Chief Hawes and two policemen remained, examining evidence.

At base camp, the change in the expedition team was palpable. Tad thought he felt some of the overall gloom directed at him. As the rest resumed their normal duties, he walked down to the riverside with his bag of clothes.

"Strange washing habits they have in Buffalo," Linda observed from the ridge above him in the late-afternoon sun.

Tad held up the rock he was using to pound a work shirt.

"More like de-creasing," he admitted, hoping he didn't sound as idiotic as he felt.

She joined him, offering a wedge of her orange while she surveyed his progress. "That shirt is coming along," she said. "But you get the same results by putting a few rocks in the washing machine, along with a load of clothes."

"Is that right?"

"Yeah." She wiped away a line of juice from her chin with the back of her hand.

"Kind of non-traditional, isn't it?" he teased. "Using a washing machine?"

"My father taught me how to do it. He says it makes all new, stiff clothes feel comfortable. Stone-washed, it's called."

"Ancient Cherokee custom?"

Linda grinned. "Oh, from way back to the dawn of time. Real sixties stuff."

"Sixties?"

"Stone-washing, tie dye, Buffy St. Marie and Bob Dylan protest songs. My father's singing voice is almost as bad as that guy's. Drives my mother crazy, but the songs are what brought them together."

"And so...you came about?"

"Eventually. You catch on quickly, Buffalo Man." She looked across the river bank. "The police will be working at Tallalla's tomb until after dark. I'm going to check on Moses. Want to come?"

"To Caleb Barker's attraction?"

"The El Dorado Diggings, yes. It's around the ridge, about a half mile walk. There are some interesting caves there too."

Maybe they both needed to get away for awhile. "I'll run these pieces of up-to date-90s grunge art to my tent. Be right back."

She giggled. He liked that sound.

When Tad plunged through the men's tent, he saw Mrs. Christie kneeling beside his cot.

She jumped up. "Tad! You startled me!"

"What are you doing, Mrs. Christie?"

"There!" she pointed to his duffle bag. "That's what I've been looking for!"

He looked down. "My clothes?"

"Yes! I'm going into town. Dr. Duncan is giving us all assignments to keep us out of the police's way. I'll get those washed for you, dear!"

"That's very nice of you, Mrs. Christie, but I've been doing my own laundry since I was ten. Mom insisted. I can also cook three decent dinners. So that I'm never a burden to society and some poor woman, she says. If she ever found out I allowed you—"

"It will be our secret then," she said, taking the bag.

Tad winced, hoping she wouldn't notice that the dirt ground into his clothes was self inflicted. He surrendered the bag to her.

"That's a good boy," she approved. "Don't worry. My spoiling will be just between us."

Tad watched her walk towards the main tent. "Since the age of ten," she said to no one in particular. "That's the price the boy has paid for his mother's TV glamor. Practically an orphan!"

Yesterday Tad might have taken comfort in Mrs. Christie's assessment to further blame his family's move to the South. Now, he laughed and shook his head. But however much he would protest, Mrs. Christie would see him as a neglected child. Well, that was her problem. He had other problems to deal with. Like his feelings for Linda Tassel. And a murder.

Tad found Linda waiting at the river. As he followed her along the cedar and pine framed trail, it widened and began to show signs of a tourist attraction ahead. As the rocky ground leveled out, he took her hand and pressed it to his face.

"Are you feeling better, Linda?" he asked quietly.

She nodded, avoiding his eyes. "And you?" she whispered.

"I'll help you put your site back together, I promise."

"Nothing will be right until we find out who did this terrible thing, Tad. And why."

They stopped. She went into his arms. It felt as natural as breathing. "Yeah," Tad agreed.

He caught the faint scent of sage from her skin. The smell of her shock and fear had obliterated it that morning, on the top of Little Mound, after she'd found Dr. Steffy's body. Tad shivered at the memory. Linda's arms massaged his back, and the welts she'd made in her fear.

He wanted to kiss her. Would she taste like sage? He'd kissed girls before. It wasn't hard. It took a little nerve, a little hope that she wouldn't turn away, that's all. He'd done it before. What was stopping him? Not any love he once thought he felt for Julie Tolliver. That perfume-soaked last letter explaining how she thought they should start "seeing other people" was now a pale memory.

What was so different about this girl and her fierce devotion to her own people, past and present? Everything was different about her. And he wanted a taste of it. He held her face in his hand, stroking her strong jawline with his thumb as he lowered his head. Yes. She was going to allow it. She was, maybe even going to kiss him back.

A blood-curdling scream startled them both.

From the rhododendron bushes behind them, a gaggle of screeching kids swooped by, running up the path. Linda laughed nervously, an echo of her reaction to the tragedy of the morning.

They took each other's hands and followed the growing number of families headed toward El Dorado. Arrow-shaped signs pointed the ways to Deadwood, Lost Boy Well, and Hang Town.

One of the arrows was stripped like a red and white candy cane. It directed visitors to the North Pole.

"That's a left-over from last year," Linda explained. "Mr. Barker tried to lure in a Christmas crowd with 'Santa's Secret Gold Hideaway.'"

Tad suppressed a smile. "Did it work?"

"I don't think so. But it wasn't much of an investment. The exhibit was the same as "Hernando De Soto's Lost Gold Mine,' except he powdered De Soto's beard and put a red cap on his head."

"What a rip-off."

Linda shrugged. "Well, none of us is perfect. And Hernando smells better powdered and giving out gifts than stealing our gold."

They rounded the last bend on the path and the main amusement area in a meadow. Great piles of red dirt sat outside a long archway with a metal sheeting roof. Tourists leaned over wooden troughs, watching the water move over red clay sediment. Along the last, more tourists were panning for gold with varying degrees of enthusiasm. Whole families were among those panning, but most of the children were playing in a Wild West stagecoach replica decorated with peeling paint decorations.

Caleb Barker stood beside an employee outfitted like a cowboy who hand pumped water along the trough to aid the gold seekers' efforts.

"May we really keep the gold we find?" a young panner asked.

"Every ounce, young fellow," Caleb Barker proclaimed magnanimously. "My gift to you for visiting this little slice of Georgia history."

"Aw, this is boring. I like the snake better," the boy's friend said, putting down his pan.

"Riches don't come to the likes of him, folks," Caleb boomed over the small crowd. "Yes, indeed! Riches come to the patient and persistent, like this little lady, Linda Tassel, who battled that snake just this morning!"

"Did you?" the bored boy asked.

"How do you think Old Moses lost his fang?" the man answered for her. "Yes, never a dull moment here at El Dorado! Don't forget to visit all the caves of history...from the melting snows of the Ice Age to the rugged and resourceful Dahlonega miners! There's still gold in these here hills! Watch for yourselves on TV tonight. And tell your friends to come up and see us!"

Tad heard Linda sigh. "Good afternoon, Mr.Barker," she said.

Caleb Barker waved. "Come on over here, Linda, Tad. Give the folks some tips on treasure hunting! Oh, now, as I live and breathe...what have you got there, little missy?"

A mud splattered girl who reminded Tad of his sister Maggie dug deep in her mining pan. "Look, Mommy, it's a ring!" she proclaimed. "A diamond ring!"

Caleb came to her side. He studied the rhinestone children's ring as if he had a jeweler's loupe at his eye. "Why Linda, I think your Queen of the Cherokees has visited our humble gold diggings!"

To Tad's surprise, Linda smiled as she examined the dime store bauble that the little girl placed in her palm. "Tallalla was an artist, not a queen," she told the little girl who stared up at her, wide-eyed. "But I think she would be proud to wear such a pretty ring."

She returned it and the little girl ran off to show her treasure to her friends playing on the stagecoach.

"Watch that quicksilver, folks!" Mr. Barker said as he bade farewell to this remaining audience, "Particles of gold stick to the quicksilver! Happy hunting!"

As they walked toward the sign that proclaimed "Moses's Den, the big man took hold of Tad's shoulder. "Well, what do you think of the diggings thus far?" he asked.

"It's interesting," Tad tried.

"Interesting? Interesting? Look here, son. This is a barrel rocker, this a long-tom mining. You're looking at history. The Spanish used this equipment process five hundred years ago!"

Linda folded her arms. "And did the Spanish deposit jewelry in their diggings?" she asked.

"Aw, I had a surplus of that supply of birthstone ring at the gift shop. Ain't little girls born in April any more?"

Linda shook her head. "You're both smarter and sweeter than you act, Mr. Barker."

He let out a grunt in response. "If I'm so smart, why ain't I rich?"

She shrugged. "Too sweet."

The big man pulled off his floppy hat and scratched his balding head. "Now, there's no sense in ruining a man's reputation, missy." He brought the hat back down over his ears. "Now, you came to check on Moses, I'm thinking?"

"Your company is a good bonus," Linda said diplomatically. "And I'm sure Tad would enjoy a tour of the rest of the entertainments."

The big man grunted again. "This way." He grabbed a battery-powered lantern from a line of them waiting to assist visitors through a mine shaft now closed with a rope across its entrance and a sign proclaiming "Last tour 3:15 PM."

Inside, Tad was surprised to enter a world different from the worn and gaudy displays. The shaft was hewn deep. Its red clay walls framed gaping holes left over from the area's gold rush days.

"When were these tunnels dug?" Tad asked.

"1830s and 40s. The miners found gold in fissure veins of quartz."

Tad saw evidence of the shiny metal in the minimum-lighted walls. It made a dramatic effect.

"It wasn't until the spectacular finds in California that Georgians took up their equipment and headed west. These hollowed out remains of shafts and natural caves are what's left," Caleb said, all his bluster gone and a sadness taking over his storytelling voice.

This place wasn't so different than where Linda toiled, Tad realized, except for the things the earlier people left behind embedded in its depths.

At the end of one passageway Caleb Barker flipped a switch. A deep gash in the ground, now more rock than clay, was illuminated. "Welcome to Lost Boy Well," he explained.

Tad peered over the rim down unfathomable depths.

"Watch your step," their guide advised. "It's ready to take a few more victims since the little tyke was lost."

"I'm surprised it hasn't taken any of your visitors."

"Oh, it's safe enough. You can hear more about its history on special ghost tours at night. Even your Dr. Duncan took that one."

"Did he?" Linda asked. "I can't imagine that."

"Back in the first year. You were not the high and mighty scholar back then, either, Linda Tassel. You and your clan brother did your dance for us, as I recall."

"Guli and I danced as your guests, sir."

"And then he talked you out of working for me?"

"No, sir. That was my decision."

Tad had the feeling that Linda and Caleb Barker had this discussion before, and would again. He admired her serene patience with the man.

"I won't be bothering you about it today. Not today, young ones," he said sadly.

Tad was grateful for the warm squeeze of Linda's hand before Mr. Barker spoke again.

"W. C., he'll do his best. And you'll get to return to your little artist woman, Linda. I told him I'd hold him to that."

"Why, Mr. Barker," Linda whispered.

The man grunted and led them down yet another corridor in this underground maze. "Almost there. Found my Moses a nice plump mouse this morning to help him through his own ordeal." He noticed Tad's new boots. "Better footwear," the big man approved. "Don't reckon either of your ankles would have any appeal to him now."

He stopped, flicked a switch, and a tableau of treasures was illuminated in a small amphitheater space. Painted sculptures decorated with elaborate feathered headdresses, earrings, and masks abounded. So did overflowing clay pots of jewelry, golden jaguar and serpent figurines.

"More Aztec than Mississippian," Linda commented softly at Tad's ear.

"Got to catch their attention." Caleb Barker retorted. "That's what you fancy educators don't understand. This is El Dorado, fabled city of gold! A place of imagination, missy! Of gold, treasure!"

"Gold. The sweat of the sun, a sacred gift," Linda said evenly.

"I tell them that, too. Sure, it's all part of a great story. You folks are the legitimate archeologists, historians, and I'm some side show of the 'wild east?' Well, Georgia was wild once, and I know human nature. You don't draw them in with pipe stems and wampum, but with gold!"

"And snakes?" Tad asked.

"Sure? Didn't you hear that kid? No attention for panning, but he got himself a little history lesson when he was in here looking at—"

Suddenly Caleb Barker made gasping noises. He rushed up to the terrarium display flanked by a pair of two-headed monster figures with topaz-colored eyes. He flung aside the broken-locked top.

"Moses," he crooned quietly. "What did they do to you?"

Caleb gently lifted the body. The mouse thumped out of a gaping hole. He then looked past Tad to Linda, standing stone still at Tad's side.

"You didn't do this," Caleb Barker told her.

"I caused him to be brought here," she said in a strange monotone.

"No, you did not, missy. I did. You hear me, Linda Tassel?"

"I allowed you to take him from Little Mound."

"Now, I don't recall asking your permission. He came home. I took him back home."

She took a step closer. "Poor Moses."

"You got that right, little lady. Poor Moses. Not you. Not any member of your family, you hear? Just Moses."

Tad didn't understand what was going on between them. He followed Linda closer to the terrarium. He gently grazed her back with his fingers. The snake had been neatly sliced in half. The act was planned, he thought, right to the terrarium's top replaced. He glanced down at the dirt floor. It was full of the footprints of many tourists. Who could have done this? Why?

"I didn't think to post a guard," Caleb Barker said. "Who would want to kill Moses?"

Linda turned away. Tad followed.

"Wait up," Caleb called after them. I'm going to close down the place until we have a ceremony. In the morning, Linda, do you hear me? We'll have a ceremony, all right?"

Linda nodded, but she didn't turn back.

Chapter Ten

Even Mrs. Christie was out of sorts as she plunged their mashed potatoes onto their dinner plates.

"No softball game tonight, Dr. Hamilton says," she groused. "A game would be the best thing. Dr. Steffy would want us to play. We need to do what we always do."

"The power of ritual," Linda agreed with a tentative smile.

"My bunion's telling me we've got a frog-strangling rain coming up, too," Mrs. Christie complained to the next dig volunteer in line.

Tad and Linda found seats. When he noticed her pushing her potatoes around on her plate, Tad dug into one of the multiple pockets in his vest. "Might go well," he suggested, pulling out the item and slicing it easily with his table knife.

"What is that?"

"Kielbasa. Polish delicacy in these parts." He offered her a sliver. "Try?"

She tasted. "Good," she approved.

Later in the mess tent, everyone gathered around a small television. The ten o'clock news led with Dr. Steffy's murder, the horror of it offset by testimonials of his colleagues, led by Dr. Hamilton. Kelsey Doyle enlarged the story when she spoke of the dig and its group of dedicated professionals and volunteers, and how they were working to save a piece of an ancient civilization before the dam project flooded the Allatoona River.

Everyone admired the glimpses of Bill Steele's arial photography of the dig site, views which revealed the hilly landscape dotted with cave openings on both sides of the river.

They nodded in approval at interviews with townspeople, who said they'd gotten along well with the academics over the last three summers, and were happy for their business, from massive local grocery orders to coffee shop visits to bowling.

"That's funny," Mrs. Christie said softly. "I order all our groceries trucked in from the Atlanta food co-op that the university uses, not the local grocery stores."

"And we're hardly starving enough for that much in our snack runs," Bill Steele agreed. "Me, I'm disappointed that the proprietors of local watering holes have not even said they'd miss my miserable poker hands."

Tad watched his mom's interview with Dr. Hamilton. "How has this young Native

American woman become a dig site supervisor?" she asked.

"The hard way, Ms. Doyle. She earned it."

"Dig boss sounds like Clint Eastwood," Mrs. Christie observed.

"Oh, no," Erla Wingdale protested. "Tough but tender. More like Sean Connery."

"No new nicknames!" Dr. Duncan commanded.

Tad grinned at Linda. The team almost seemed like its old self. He hoped the good natured camaraderie would continue.

And then the next part of the news story appeared.

Linda appeared on screen, answering Kelsey Doyle's questions. The camera focused on her earnest face, her quill earrings, her expressive hands. As she smiled that smile that Tad knew had been for him, her quiet voice faded as images of the sheriff's men swarming over her dig, and a menacing single-fanged pit viper got his close-up, courtesy of his proud owner, Caleb Barker, inviting one and all to visit El Dorado and pan for gold. Tad winced. Who would have thought that hours from that moment, Moses himself would be the victim?

Then the screen filled with stock images of past demonstrations by Native Americans, protesting dam projects, burning tires and blocking highways as an unseen male narrator turned up the fear meter.

The team sat in stunned silence as the news segment ended. And it wasn't over yet.

A late-breaking story interrupted the weather report. A photograph of some Cherokee demonstrators flashed on the screen, with news that four of them were being sought for questioning in the death of Dr. Steffy. One was Linda's clan brother Guli. Tad recognized the other three guys— Guli's companions.

Finally, the evening news ended. Dr. Duncan rose to snap off the television.

"I'm going into town," Bill Steele said, his jaw set in anger. "That is, if my tires haven't been slashed. Anybody coming?"

"I think we should all stay here," Dr. Duncan advised.

The photographer flung his leather jacket over his shoulder. "Isolate ourselves? Why?"

"To present a united front."

"Circle the wagons, you mean?" Erla Wingdale took up the debate. "We've already got those blasted bulldozers crowding in on us, on our work."

"We may as well pick up our shovels and help Peterson dig his damned lake!" Pete Lowery agreed.

"Remember the two cultures joining together on shared land? What happened to that?" Anne Kane asked, looking at Linda with sympathy. "Bill's right. The last thing we should do is isolate ourselves."

"It's for his own protection," Dr. Duncan maintained.

Harold Brock stood. "Protection from whom? Most of Cartersville wants the lake. And the Indians are on the run from the police," he added. "I don't understand. Dr. Steffy never had a bad word about anyone. He always stood up for free speech at town meetings. It's can't be the Cherokee behind this."

Bill Steele turned to Dr. Hamilton. "What do you say, boss? You sign our paychecks."

"Go on," Dr. Hamilton said in a weary voice. "Don't cheat."

"I never do."

Tad turned his attention from the group to realize that Linda was gone. He pulled Fred Christie's fedora hat low over his eyes, grabbed two flashlights and left the tent.

He walked the dig site trails, trying to keep the sound of the river within hearing distance. He didn't want to humiliate himself by getting lost. Finally, he found Linda sitting by the Allatoona's banks, staring into his silvery depths. Foolish Boy was at her feet. Linda's dog lifted his head, recognized Tad, then went back to his position.

Linda didn't even do that.

"Hey," Tad said softly. "You forgot your regulation flashlight." He placed one at her feet. She didn't move.

"Aren't you afraid of missing the slither of one of Moses' friends down here?" he tried.

"Cottonmouth," she said softly.

"Huh?"

"Cottonmouth is the snake that likes being near water."

"I see. And…as deadly?"

"Oh, yes."

"And you're not afraid?"

"No."

Good, Tad thought. She was still speaking to him, even if her gaze did not stray from water gurgling over the rocks. He sat beside her. "Since my new boots, we're an invincible team, eh?"

"We're all on a team, Tad. I know I am the stranger among you, but I thought the team part was what your mother was interested in. All of us learning from what the Mound Builders left us. She went up in that plane with Mr. Steele. She interviewed most of us."

"The longer documentary will tell more of the dig story, Linda, you'll see."

"Dr. Hamilton thought she understood the project. He trusted her. He permitted total access."

"She is interested. I don't know what happened," he admitted.

"Why did she show Moses as if he was some demon? Why show different Indian people—Mohawk and Seneca people, with different grievances, burning tires and blocking highways? I liked her, Tad. I thought she cared. I feel betrayed."

Linda sounded so heartbroken. He reached for her hand. She didn't pull away. "I don't know what happened, Linda. Mom's new at this job. The producers hold more sway over what goes over the air here. That other footage didn't belong, you're right. Neither did the male voice-over. That's not like my mom's work at all."

"What do you mean?"

"If you closed your eyes and only listened, the words were a little dramatic, maybe, but not incendiary or accusing. That stock footage of other protests pumped it up, you see? My mother taught me to be on guard for tricks like that. She hates them. I'll bet she's fuming over it and raising hell."

"How could it have happened if it was her report?"

"I'll find out, I promise. Mom came from a local news station in Buffalo. She worked as head of a team of writer, producer, editor, camera crew. Every on the air broadcast was her responsibility, and she sank or swam by them. Maybe it's not the same at Current News. Maybe she doesn't have the same control. I don't know. But I'll find out."

Tad pressed the small, cold hand under his. "Aw, Linda. You're breaking my heart. Will you look at me?"

She raised her head. "That is bad manners."

"What is?"

"To look directly in a person's eyes. I had to learn to do things like that, to act white, before I could get out of the 'dummy' corner at school."

She blinked away tears. Linda seemed so comfortable in both worlds, Tad thought, even if maybe neither was comfortable with her.

"Well, I guess you'd better put me in the dummy corner now," he said.

His words were not what she expected, maybe. Tad held his arms out. Relief flooded him when she buried her head in his chest. He stroked the glossy, blunt-cut hair spilling from her bandana. Its blackness shone in the moon's light.

"I'm pretty ignorant, eh?"

"No, you're just from Buffalo."

He laughed. "That earns me your patience?"

"That, and other things."

She was flirting with him! Wasn't she? "Like what?"

She touched the first button of his shirt. "Your hat. I like your hat."

Her finger made a lazy circle around the button. It was all Tad could stand. He took the curve of her face in his and kissed her.

She returned the kiss. She tasted of the chicory coffee she had been sipping as they watched television, that and sage. The fingers he had felt strafe his back in terror after she found Dr. Steffy's mutilated body now wound through his hair until the hat she liked so much hit the ground. Tad was glad it was not two hundred years ago. He was glad Linda was not his enemy.

From his peripheral vision Tad noticed Foolish Boy's head dart up. He was about to grumble about dog chaperones when he heard a low throated snarl.

"Laying claim to our Indian Princess?"

Foolish Boy stood at attention as Bill Steele stepped out of the shadows, smelling of bourbon.

"I thought you were going into town, Mr. Steele," Tad said evenly.

"Didn't get far before the town came to me."

"What are you talking about?"

"Ask your mother."

Linda took Tad's hand. "What do you want, Mr. Steele?" she demanded.

"It's not what I want. It's what has to be since you proved such a compelling heroine."

"I do not know what you're—"

"Look, you can play your Indian games, but I need this job, not trouble, not a shut down. It's supporting two kids." Bill Steele ran a hand over his haggard face. "Dr. Steffy wants you both at base camp."

He turned abruptly and walked back down the path.

Tad and Linda looked at each other. "What's gotten into him?" Tad asked.

Linda looked crestfallen. "He has never talked to me that way. Something bad has happened."

Chapter Eleven

As they walked into camp, Tad knew Linda was right.

Mrs. Christie's eyes were sympathetic as she touched his arm. "It's only temporary, dear hearts, remember that," she said as she opened the trailer door for them.

Inside, Dr. Hamilton paced, while Rose La Vera held Linda's hand. Dr. Duncan stood by, looking lost without his clipboard.

"The phone's been ringing since the news report," Dr Hamilton finally said. "The university has been inundated with protests about sponsoring a project that is so controversial. We've heard from the Cherokee Coalition, too."

"Mr. Steele did?" Tad guessed.

"That's right. On his way into town, at gunpoint. We were on the same side of the dam issue. But now they are convinced that we've made a deal, sold out to the Peterson Company, because it has allowed us to finish our dig. Some of the threats... They are a fringe element of the coalition, I'm sure.

They are cowards who won't leave their names.

"What kind of threats?" Tad asked.

"Against the dig continuing. And, specifically, against Linda. Saying they conjured up that snake to visit the site of an apple Indian."

Tad saw a wince of pain enter Linda's eyes.

Dr. Hamilton continued. "We are very pleased with your work," he assured her. "But in the light of these new developments, and all the media attention," he drew a breath, "Linda, we'd like you to work with Dr. Gist in Atlanta for now, if that's all right with you, and your parents."

"Leave here?"

Now Dr. Hamilton winced. "We discussed other options with the university and the sheriff's department. But every other possibility involved security—a difficult proposition for an open river valley site. We're not even fenced in."

He paused. "Might you think of it as a change in assignment?"

To Tad's astonishment, Dr, Duncan took Linda's hands in his like a doting uncle. "You'll be helping us form a bridge to the next stage of our study," he said earnestly. "You'll be processing all our information, cataloguing the artifacts for display at the university. Not glamorous, I know, but important."

Dr. Hamilton continued his colleague's appeal. "Then we'll need you to form another bridge. To the Snowbird and the Qualla Boundary Cherokee, so we can decide together how best to transfer the artifacts to them."

"What about Tallalla?" she asked the men.

"That's your dig site," Dr. Duncan said firmly. "It will be closed until you return. No one will take a spoonful of dirt from there until then, I promise you."

"Thank you, sir."

The small man finally released her hands. He nodded curtly to Tad and the others and left the trailer.

Rose La Vera smiled. "This is bringing out new sides in each of us," she marveled. "Dr. Duncan was your biggest supporter in keeping you on as a member of the dig, Linda. Does that surprise you as much as it does us?"

"Yes," Linda admitted. "I thought he barely tolerated me."

"Maybe he's a little fearful of your artist friend down there," Dr. Hamilton said. "Don't worry, Linda. There will be time for you to finish. After things calm down."

"That's good." She nodded. "I will go and pack my things now."

Linda didn't meet anyone's eyes before she turned and walked out.

Tad watched Foolish Boy's shadow join hers "Dr. Hamilton," he said, "Do you think things will calm down?"

"I don't know, son," he said.

"I'd like your permission to remain Linda's assistant. I think I could better serve the dig from Atlanta, too."

Dr. Hamilton offered his hand. "We'll miss your fancy footwork on the softball field," he said.

* * *

Tad unpinned Maggie's drawings from the wall of the men's tent near his cot. When he pulled out his duffel bag, he found its zipper open. He looked over the items inside. The box of chocolate truffles from his mother had been opened. Smears of chocolate were everywhere, the gold foil wrappings, smashed. A creepy feeling rode up his arms as he cleared the mess.

He lay his sister's drawings in the bag first. He looked around for his stone-washed clothes then remembered that Mrs. Christie had takenthem to the town laundromat.

Suddenly the flap of the men's tent opened and there stood the dig's cook herself, with her hair tied up in curlers and her long chenille robe fluttering in the night air.

"Tad! Thank goodness! Linda's going to phone her father to take her home!"

"Tonight?"

"Yes! Go to her! Stay with her!"

"Yes, ma'am. Where did she—"

"The trailer, dear boy, where the phones are!"

Tad pulled his duffle bag high on his shoulder. Mrs. Christie took his face between her small, strong hands. "Take care of each other, you hear?" she whispered, before pulling him down and planting a kiss on his forehead.

He found Foolish Boy and Linda sitting on the ground outside the dimly-lit trailer. Linda's head was resting on her propped-up backpack.

He crouched beside her. "Hey."

"It's locked. And I have already surrendered all my keys."

"How did that go? Was Dr. Duncan glad to get them back?"

"No. He was so kind. Promised me that no one would touch Tallalla. He said that he respected my work. Everyone is nice when you leave, I guess."

Geeze Louise, Tad thought. We're both going to be bawling soon. "Linda. You don't have to call your father. Mom left me my car. I'll drive you home, if you want to go tonight."

"It is too late, too far."

He lifted his backpack. "Not if I stay over at your place. I mean, if your family will allow it. If not, I can sleep in the car. Then we can go to Atlanta together. I'm still your assistant, and still on my one-week probation. We need to convince a bunch of nervous university officials not to shut the dig down before you finish Tallalla's story. Is that worth putting up with me a little longer?"

Linda smiled. "Yes, it is."

Chapter Twelve

Their flashlights found Tad's car. It had been washed to gleaming outside and spotless inside. He wished his mother hadn't seen to that. He was looking for ways to give the lumbering old maroon '82 Mercedes 240D some character. Her efforts weren't helping. A shiny fresh waxed finish was not the latest in grunge fashion. He opened the spacious trunk and threw in their packs, then opened the rear door.

"I think Foolish Boy will be comfortable back here."

"More than he has ever been in his life," Linda said, staring at the lighted interior and its palomino leather seats. "This is your car?"

"Not exactly 'me' is it? Aww, it comes from having a news hound in the family, full of accident statistics on new drivers and the safest rated cars. Mom swears by this old Mercedes. And my dad is a tree shade mechanic—always tinkering and keeping it running. My dad can take an engine, rebuild it, and get another hundred thousand miles out of it. After Mom got her new job, I got her '82, and she bought a newer '88. It's even bigger. And green." He made a sour face. "I would have preferred a GTO, vintage Mustang, but with her 'safety first' philosophy, I could have gotten stuck with an army surplus tank."

Linda smiled. "I think your mother is very wise. About some things," she added before falling silent again.

As they drove along back country roads, Tad noticed route signs almost swallowed by runaway green vines of kudzu. His dad had told him about the lush ground cover imported from Japan to stop soil erosion. It had become part of much Southern lore. But he couldn't prompt any of it from Linda. Maybe she had other things on her mind.

"Are you trying to figure out how to explain why I'm bringing you home in the middle of the night?" he finally asked.

"Among other things."

"Leave me to bring them over with my natural Buffalo charm."

"Okay. Make a right at the flashing light ahead."

They watched a young fox scamper out of the way of the Mercedes' high beams.

What did he think he was doing? Linda's family would eat him alive. He felt her warmth as she moved closer. He wished 'the barge' as he called his parents' gift, was better for snuggling as it was for safety.

"You're not going to make this easy for me, are you?"

"Hmmm?"

"I want to know more about your family and friends. After all, you've already met my parents, and when we get to Atlanta—"

"Tad?"

"Yeah?"

"I have never been to Atlanta."

"On your own, you mean? Don't worry, I'm new myself, but I'm used to cities."

"Ever. Never, ever."

"But you only live a couple of hours away."

"I know."

"Linda, if you get the scholarship to attend Morris next year—"

"My parents have not yet agreed that I should go. We moved off the reservation only three years ago. To Cartersville...a town of a gas station, a general store, and a post office, all in the same building. Atlanta...that is the moon to us."

"Did you tell Dr. Hamilton this when he re-assigned us there?"

"No. I was so stunned at being sent away. I know Dr. Hamilton is trying to keep me involved in the dig, and the possibility of finishing my work."

He reached over at touched Linda's arm lightly. "Hey. Don't worry. I've survived Buffalo blizzards. Convincing your parents that Peachtree Street won't kill you can't be too hard, can it?"

"We'll find out," she said. "We're here."

The big white clapboard house was older and in more rugged shape than the graceful 1912 vintage house his parents had purchased in the Inman Park section of Atlanta. Linda's place was on a main road, but set back from it by a lane lined in old hickory trees. Tad counted five brick chimneys. Four Greek-style columns still held up double front porches. Six-over-six paned windows contained wavy glass reflecting the moonlight. After living with house preservationists all his life, Tad knew this house was probably built before the Civil War, by slaves. Hanging from the second-story porch was a large wooden sign with painted letters he couldn't read. They reminded him of the Russian Cyrillic Alphabet.

"Cherokee," Linda said softly. "Our linguist Sequoyah put the sounds of our language into symbols."

"What does it say?"

"The Cherokee Phoenix. It is an art gallery. We live behind and above it."

Tad got out of the car and opened the back door. Foolish Boy leapt out to a welcoming chorus of barks and yelps from the back of the house.

"Foolish Boy's sisters," Linda explained with a smile. "They will go out on a grand frolic in the woods and not be back for hours."

Tad opened the trunk and took out Linda's backpack. She reached for his.

"Better leave it there until I find out if I'm welcome."

"You are welcome, Tad."

"After my mother's report?"

"They did not see it."

"How do you know that?"

"No television."

"You don't have a television?"

She shrugged. "We used to. It only received two channels out here. Then it broke. My father kept looking for a place that would repair it, and when he finally did, the man said he'd have to send away for parts. By that time, we decided it was nicer around the house without it."

They both turned when a porch light came on. A man opened the big front door. His blond hair was tied back in a ponytail and he was dressed in faded work jeans and a calico shirt. His light eyes shone when he saw Linda. He opened his arms and she flew into them.

Tad stood in the darkness as they talked. The man listened intently, his eyes pained and compassionate. Tad wondered who he was. Then Linda pulled him over to the car.

"Tad, this is my father, James."

James Tassel held out his hand. "Glad to have you, Tad," he said, grinning in a way that made his whole face look boyish, even with the silver that Tad could now see in his hair at the temples. Linda didn't look anything like this man. Tad couldn't find his voice.

Linda's father took the bag from the trunk. "Come in, come in. Theda made nut bread. Wouldn't let the rest of us touch it. She always knows when Linda's coming home."

Tad stopped Linda on the porch once the tall blond man had gone inside.

"Linda. Your father's white?"

She opened her eyes in mock surprise. "He is?" She laughed. "We tried to hide him in a closet. Did not work. Got drummed off the reservation."

"What?"

She rolled her eyes. "I'm teasing, Tad! Remember those first marriages among the Snowbird I told you about? That's why I have two names, a Cherokee and an English one, to honor both my parents. We moved off the res when my Aunt Theda needed to be close to the MS therapy center near Cartersville. We stay connected by running this branch of the tribal cooperative arts store."

Tad noticed that a section of the porch steps was covered in planks and ribbed rubber sheeting for wheelchair accessibility. The trail continued inside.

The old house was rich in unpainted chestnut flooring, and woodwork. The ceilings were high in the two front rooms that faced the road. Tad saw display cases full of beaded jewelry, pottery, sculpture, and baskets. The painted plaster walls were lined with paintings.

Linda led him on. The back of the house was a lower ceiling crazy quilt of add-on structures, with the trail of rubber path running through gradual inclines and declines.

They came to a large room containing overstuffed couches and chairs and a platform rocker whose back and seat were woven cane. Bookcases covered two walls, even winding around the windows. Most of the shelves held worn looking hardback and softcover volumes, but some displayed pots and masks. Nothing matched, but gathered around a deep hearthstone fireplace, everything looked somehow right.

Seated at the end of one of the sofas was a small woman bent over what looked like cloth made of tiny jewels. She raised her head and Tad saw huge eyes behind her round glasses and a face full of mischief.

"Grandmother Delores Longknife, this is Tad," Linda announced.

The woman reached out her hand. Tad felt calloused fingers take his in a firm shake. "And this is my granddaughter's festival dancing cape," she told him, holding up the garment studded with quills and beadwork. The glass beads were what gave it its jeweled appearance. His eyes traced the swirling roses and wind designs.

"Beautiful," was all he could think to say.

Linda's grandmother nodded. Her eyeglasses slipped to the tip of her nose as she regarded him over them. "You will come to the Harvest Festival," she said.

"Uh, great."

Delores Longknife looked over his head to Linda and her father. Get the boy to sleep now," she told them. "He is tired, and far from home."

She didn't know the half of it, Tad thought, except that maybe, somehow, she did. He watched her pick up her magnificent project and trudge down a hallway.

As Tad turned, he saw James Tassel disappear up a narrow back staircase. Linda pulled out a convertible bed from one of the room's sofas as her chin pointed to doors off the living room. "Bath, then my Aunt Theda's room. Down that hallway is my grandparents' side of the house. My parents and I have our bedrooms upstairs. You'll meet everybody in the morning."

Her father appeared again, his arms laden with pillows, blanket and fresh towels that he placed at the foot of the guest bed.

"Thank you, sir," Tad said.

James Tassel smiled warmly. "Chestnut bread at eight," he said, before soundlessly disappearing up the stairs again.

Linda shook her head. "We think he was once a panther," she said. "Or a cat burglar."

"Linda, neither your father or grandmother asked what I'm doing here."

She frowned. "That would be bad manners. You are a guest, and a tired one. See you in the morning, Tad," she said, reaching up to kiss him.

He took her waist and brought her closer. She felt wonderfully warm in his arms. "I'm not that tired," he whispered at her ear.

She giggled but pulled away. "My grandmother would not approve of any more activity. No one stays up later than she does."

"And I should watch my own manners with a grandmother who's invited me to the Harvest Festival."

Linda caressed his cheek before she scaled the stairs, disappearing. There, Tad thought. She had silent movement in common with the man who looked more like his father than hers.

During the night Tad was awakened by whispers. He raised his head and listened through the opened window, past the night's crickets, the toad's sad trill. He made out Linda's hushed voice.

The deeper toned voice was familiar too. He could only hear a few disjointed words among the whips and hisses of consonants.

They were arguing. He rose from his sofa bed and walked to the back screened door.

He didn't see anyone in the warm summer night, relieved by a blowing breeze through the nearby stand of pine. His eyes scanned past the porch into the darkness beyond.

He didn't see anyone. And the voices had silenced.

The clouds overhead swirled in the darkness, their edges illuminated by the moon's light. Storm weather. Mrs. Christie's bunions were right. If it rained, the whole dig's progress would be halted. Maybe Linda wouldn't feel as bad about being reassigned to Atlanta.

The moon escaped from its cloud cover and he saw her. She was standing by a strange looking structure that reminded Tad of a scaffold in the darkness. She was in a white nightgown, with a red-fringed shawl draped over her shoulders. From out of the shadows of the weird scaffolding, another figure appeared, with a shadow much bigger than Linda's. And a voice Tad recognized.

Guli Whitepath. The man the police were looking for.

Linda gestured towards the pines. Is that where Guli had come from? Were his buddies there? She seemed to be urging Guli to go. Tad leaned against the screen door.

"I heard you were scratched by a briar, sister," the big guy said.

Linda touched her throat. "Yes."

"I will speak to the little men, the sons of Thunder. I will ask them to take the ghost inside, to adorn themselves. I will say the formula for you, and for the sister of your mother, who might sicken if you are too strong for *inada's* ghost."

"Thank you, my brother."

"You are strong. A warrior."

He dug into his jeans' pocket and pulled out a cord necklace. He placed it over Linda's head as he began a soft chant, directing its words to the night sky. A rumble of thunder answered. Linda's hands hung at her sides as she stared upward at the falling rain. Tad found it all strangely hypnotic. Until the flash of knives.

He plunged through the doorway, yelling.

Chapter Thirteen

Tad regretted he had not gone out for his high school football team before he tucked his head and barreled into Guli's gut.

He heard the metallic clink of the knives falling against stone as he and Guli landed on the ground. He punched and kicked at a guy who probably had thirty pounds on him.

"Tad, stop it!" he dimly heard Linda cry.

Guli fisted his t-shirt and muttered something in Cherokee before landing a blow. Tad tasted blood.

"Both of you, stop!" Linda yelled, as the rain fell harder.

But it was the blare of sirens that ended the fight.

Guli got to his knees, looking frantically toward the pine woods, illuminated by a flash of lightning. Linda grabbed his rolled-up shirtsleeve. "No. They'll shoot."

He pushed her away and took off. A police officer ordered a halt.

Linda sank down. "They will kill him," she said in a dull voice that Tad never wanted to hear again.

So he took off after him, blocking the policeman's sights.

The distance between them closed. By then Tad could only hear the pumping of his heart, the squash of his footfalls on the slippery ground. He sprang low, as if Guli was second base, and brought him down.

"Good work, hero," Guli muttered in disgust as the policemen caught up.

They pressed his hands behind his back and cuffed them. He didn't appear to be listening as Chief Hawes read him his rights. His glance only shifted toward Tad when Hawes asked Linda, who was standing between her father and a sweet-faced woman who Tad figured was her mother, if Linda wanted to press any charges.

"No, sir," she said clearly.

Guli lifted his head higher, glaring at Tad before the police led him to a patrol car.

Tad sat outside on the front porch wooden rocker while Chief Hawes finished his questioning of the Tassel family, there inside the business part of the Cherokee Phoenix house. He stared out into the relentless rainfall. A frog strangler, Mrs. Christie had called it. It was that, all right, but he was too tired to smile.

He kept playing back the events of the night in his head, trying to make sense of them. But this was no video game. And nothing eased the weight on his chest.

W.C. Hawes finally emerged from the store, easing the screen door closed. He stood over Tad.

"Steal many bases last season?"

Tad continued staring out at the rain. "Fifty-six."

"How's the lip?"

"All right," Tad lied. It stung.

"Guns were drawn. I don't expect I need to say how ill-considered that run and tackle was."

"No, sir."

"And it'd be a waste of breath to ask if you'd like to file your own complaint against Guli Whitepath?"

"I guess he's got all he can handle right now."

"You got that right." He drew up a willow chair and sat beside Tad. "Was he going after Linda with those knives?"

"I guess not."

"But it's what you thought, why you knocked him down?"

Tad stared ahead.

"It doesn't look good. If the shotgun is traced to him or his three pals who headed for the hills, we might have a gang. 'The Cherokee Four' the hotheads on TV are calling them already. Young Guli was trying to join his friends, I suspect, but stopped off to visit his clan sister. Colorful."

Tad leaned his head on his outstretched arms.

"Have you got the card I gave you at the dig?" the police chief asked.

"Yes, sir."

"Good. Linda's got one too now. She told me you're going to Atlanta tomorrow. Her father says you'll be together. I need to know where you are, Tad. Both of you. At all times."

"Chief Hawes?"

"Yes?"

"Do you think Guli killed Dr. Steffy?"

"Not time to think yet. I'm following leads. Motives. Suspicious behavior. Sometimes we get jerked around by them. So far evidence points to young Whitepath neatly. Maybe too neatly. We even found one of his ceremonial knives near where he and his friends were camping near the university's dig, conveniently smeared with Dr. Steffy's blood. We've got his history of demonstrating against the dam, and against the university's deal with Peterson's company. His desperation was showing. Even shouting at his clan sister. Got several testimonies about that. Yours being conspicuously absent. You got a memory problem, boy?"

"He didn't yell at Dr. Steffy."

"But I asked about any arguments, remember? His clan sister didn't mention it either, in our first interview. When you were both pretty shook up. That's how I excuse it."

"What happens now, sir?"

"Guli Whitepath's got no prior record. Looks like we're got an amateur perpetrator, with motives personal if we throw in a little scorned boyfriend thanks to you. And political. We've got opportunity, an unverifiable alibi, and associative evidence. The boy himself added sudden flight. Might make it to trial."

"Unless he's been framed."

"You have any ideas along those lines?"

"No, sir," Tad admitted. "But Linda will never believe Guli is a murderer."

"Yeah, I got that much out of her." The chief rubbed his knees. "Well, better head out and get some useful work done."

"What kind of work, sir?"

"Getting a look at your mother's unedited footage, for one thing. She got to a lot of those townspeople before we did. Fresh reactions while we were still dusting for fingerprints and clearing the body. Wish she was a detective and not a nosy newswoman."

"She's on your side, chief. This may be nothing but—"

"What?"

"When we were watching my mom's report together at base camp, two of the women noticed something strange, something the town grocer said."

"The grocer? Dell Seeger?"

"He said he'd gotten a lot of business from the dig, that he would miss. But our

132

cook has staples brought in from Atlanta. From the university's food co-op."

"He didn't mean snacks, bottles of Coke for dance and poker nights?"

"No, sir. He said groceries."

"Somebody's lying. How interesting. I know Dell Seeger. Good supply of night crawlers and fishing flies out back of the store. His books are exact to the penny. I wonder how the university's books are?"

"You believe Guli might not have killed Dr. Steffy, sir?"

"Let's say I'm staying alert. Because young Whitepath has not been obliging enough to confess and save the good taxpayers some money."

"Did you expect him to?"

"Almost. It's just that neat. Fanatics usually do confess, citing a higher power's directive. You know, God or the Devil made them do it, especially with ritual killing. And they don't stop their flight from the law to cure a clan sister of a curse."

The detective put his hand on Tad's shoulder. "Listen to me, son. That little girl is plenty mad at the law right now. But I don't want you two off on your own, understand? You've got my number. You think of anything, wonder about anyone, you give me a call, hear?"

"Yes, sir. Thanks."

"And, Tad?"

"Sir?"

"The Cherokee have got themselves some fine Indian lawyers. You have not tackled Guli Whitepath onto death row. Not even here in Georgia. You tell your mama that, hear?"

Tad watched the patrol car's lights disappear over the ridge. He wondered if he should crawl into the back seat of his car for the rest of the night. Maybe Foolish Boy, when he was done with his night escapades with his sisters, would crawl in with him and keep the dampness away.

He heard Linda's voice from beyond the screen door. "Come in now," she said.

"He turned. You sure?"

She sighed, pulling her red shawl around her shoulders gracefully, like she did everything, and set down a small purple glassed oil lamp.

"Beautiful," Tad said.

"Guli's work."

She sat on the wicker chair in the lamp's warm glow.

"Linda, I thought he was going to hurt you."

"I know," she said softly. "I know that's how it looked to you. That is why I want you to listen to me, now. Remember when Mr. Barker said that snakes are like supernaturals to us?"

"Yes."

"Guli is studying to be a *Kv ni a ka ti*— a holy person, a healer. He would not follow his friends into hiding until he performed the sacred formula for Moses being injured, and then killed. He is trying to keep me well." She breathed in deeply. "Wellness is harmony of body, mind, and spirit for us, Tad. We were performing a ritual, because I violated a taboo."

"What taboo?"

"Causing a mutilation of a supernatural spirit, loved by the Thunder people. There is a fear that the ghost of Moses will seek vengeance on me, or on a weaker member of my family, like my Aunt Theda, if I am strong enough to fight the ghost sickness."

Tad was almost too stunned to speak. "Linda… you believe in this stuff?"

She frowned. "My beliefs are still being formed. I honor my clan brother's courage and care."

"His knives? What was with the knives?"

"Our ceremonies are fluid, changeable. Guli works with elements that change. He makes beautiful things with molten glass. He hammers metals into his knives. He was trying to get a spark between the knives, I think. To simulate lightning."

"Lightning."

"Hear me, Tad. What is important is my clan brother's sacrifice for me. For my family. It must not be a sacrifice of his life."

135

Tad heaved a sigh. "I guess we've got our work cut out for us then."

"What you mean 'we,' pale face?"

Tad smiled, then winced. "Don't make me laugh," he warned. "It hurts when I laugh."

"Oh, I forgot." She pulled a small tin from a pocket woven into her shawl. "Aunt Theda's best healing ointment. Now go to bed. We'll need all the Buffalo charm you can muster in the morning, Taddeusz."

Chapter Fourteen

Tad woke to the sound of soft chipping. Daylight was filtering in through the soft lace curtains of the living room. He pulled on his jeans and walked out onto the wide wooden porch that stretched across the back of the rambling rear of the Tassel home. The early morning light was beautiful and rain fresh, full of promise that Tad didn't feel inside him.

The back yard's expanse of red and purple anemone and trilliums was broken by rock paths and herb and vegetable gardens, fenced high enough to keep out wildlife intruders from the forest beyond. There were two small outbuildings and a large barn.

The scaffolding contraption he'd barely seen in the darkness did not seem so ominous now. It was more like a complex, single-seat swing, set up next to an above ground pool.

Beyond the pool was underbrush of rhododendron bushes and honeysuckle vines, before the wall of pine that Guli had tried to disappear into the night before. Tad heaved a sigh, wondering if he would have made it. Even for a big guy, he moved fast.

At one end of the porch, Tad saw neatly stacked baskets like the ones Linda used at Little Mound. A few of them held burlap sacks of materials— cane, hickory strips, vines.

A breeze set the platform rocker—twin to the one Tad had seen in the living room—creaking. The door beside it opened and a short white-haired man came out. He wore grey slacks and a red chamois cloth shirt. The man had a yellow calico bandana tied around his head, worn in a simpler style than Linda wore hers. When he saw Tad he raised his hand in greeting.

Tad walked across the porch to the old man's side. "Good morning. You must be Linda's grandfather."

"*Wadan, ungilis*i," the man replied.

Tad hadn't thought of the possibility that any of Linda's relatives didn't speak English. He smiled. It didn't hurt. That ointment had worked wonders on his broken lip. "Guess we need a translator, huh?"

The old man grunted and sat in the rocker, motioning for Tad to take the stool beside it. He did. Now the Cherokee man reached into a box and pulled out a leather strop. He handed one end to Tad. Then he took a knife from the box beside it.

"You sharpening? Want me to hold the strop tight, sir?" Tad asked, gesturing.

He nodded.

"Sure. Listen. I'm wracking my brain for some of Linda's Cherokee, but all I can think of is the stuff she yells at Foolish Boy. Wolf...*waya*—I know that one!"

The old man smiled and nodded.

"Not much for starting a conversation, though."

Mr. Longknife finished his sharpening and took the strop from Tad's hand. "*Wa-to, ungilisi*," he said. His voice was even and calm, with only a hint of scratchiness.

"*Wa-to*. That's thank you, isn't it? Linda said that to Mr. Barker, when he yanked us out of the pit. I don't know how much Linda is going to tell you about that. After Dr. Steffy, and that snake, and Guli Whitepath getting arrested last night, what a mess. How am I going to convince you all to allow us to head down to Atlanta today?"

Mr. Longknife nodded politely, took a wooden form from one of his boxes, and started carving.

Tad sat up higher on the stool, watching. "Looks like you've got a mask started, huh? What's coming through now? Horns... cool! Did you ever go to the dig site, sir? The team found masks there, too. Booger masks, right? Linda told me about them."

Linda's grandfather went on with his patient carving. Tad felt at ease with his gentle, serene presence. It was like Linda's own.

Their lack of knowledge of each other's languages helped loosen Tad's own thoughts as he watched life enter the wood. "Linda, she loves that dig site, Mr. Longknife," he confided. "And she loves that Tallalla woman.

"I wanted to help her. Now I've helped put her clan brother in jail. Do you think I can make it up to her? Well, I've got to try. That's why we need to go to Atlanta, together. My family would love to host her. But I have to talk with Linda this morning, so we can make our case together. This is important. Too important for me to mess up."

The man tested his knife with the edge of his leathery finger.

"We have to earn our way back to her Little Mound site, Mr. Longknife, by finding out who killed Dr. Steffy. Especially since I freaked and got Guli captured. I saw his knives, see, and I thought he was going to hurt her.

"Well, I think she's forgiven me for that. I've never met anyone like Linda...uh, Ahyoka. That's her Cherokee name, right?"

Tad saw pleasure enter the man's dark eyes.

"Took me a while to say it right. It's a pretty name. I wonder what it means."

"She who brings happiness."

Tad almost fell off the stool. "Did you say something, sir?"

"Ahyoka means 'she brings happiness.' Her parents loved each other since they were teenaged. But they waited a long time for Ahyoka to join us. So, it is a good name, yes?"

"Uh— yeah, sure."

Tad could feel the heat rising in his face. What had he said when he thought Mr. Longknife didn't understand a word of English? He struggled to rewind his own words in his head.

The silence lingered for a full minute. Finally, the old man grinned. "Well, grandson," he said. "I think Ahyoka gave you the wrong name when she called you Buffalo Man. I think I should be carving Magpie here, maybe."

Magpie, the talkative jabberer. Well, Mr. Longknife had him there, Tad thought.

The old man went back to his work. Tad looked more closely at the booger mask in his lap. "It's a buffalo," he realized.

"*Yanasi*. A woodlands' buffalo we hunted. Not the plains one, like in the movies. I dreamed the shape of this mask, all but the forehead. That came when Ahyoka told me of you."

"When?"

"This morning. Ahyoka is a lark, like me. Not like that owl I married."

"I met Mrs. Longknife last night. She's a neat lady."

The old man grunted softly, but his eyes betrayed pleasure in Tad's assessment of his wife. "There, then," he said, offering the mask to him.

"You want me to have this?"

"Have it. Use it."

"Thank you. You're very generous."

"But not wasteful with my generosity, like white people sometimes think us to be. Ahyoka is our dear one. We trust you. To protect her, as you travel between worlds."

"What do you mean, between worlds?"

"Red and white. Living and long gone."

"The people who built the mounds?"

"They keep secrets."

"What secrets?"

The eyes almost disappeared in folds as the old man smiled. "How do I know, grandson? That is the nature of secrets."

The door on the other end of the porch opened and Tad heard a whirring sound. A woman emerged, directing a three wheeled electric scooter with one hand. Linda's parents followed. All three wore white terrycloth robes over bathing suits.

"There you are, Tad," James Tassel said. "These are the sisters Longknife— Theda and my wife Naomi, from last night?"

Naomi Tassel smiled at his tongue-tied awkwardness. "With Theda, you have now met the lot of us," she said.

Tad stepped forward. Theda Longknife's left-handed grasp of his was warm but weak.

Her right hand didn't move from her lap. Tad wondered how far her Multiple Sclerosis had affected the fragile-looking woman. He remembered Guli's words about the weak members of Linda's family falling prey to ghost sickness. Guli had been trying to help this woman, as well as Linda last night.

Theda spoke slowly, with a slight wheeze in her voice. "We are about to indulge in our morning ritual—my kin hoist me up on that contraption and I plunge into the depths of the sea. I feel like a mermaid and so am not so grouchy the rest of the day."

Tad couldn't imagine either of the Longknife sisters grouchy, somehow. He guessed Theda was older than Linda's mother, maybe in her fifties, but her worn appearance may have been due to the ravages of MS. Had Guli performed enough to be effective before he'd barged in and ruined everything? Tad hoped so, now that he'd seen Theda's brave smile.

The woman misread the concern on his face. "You look hungry," she said. We will only take a quick dip before breakfast."

"Oh, please, take your time. I have to meet with Linda… Ahyoka, before we…ah." Now he was really stuck.

"Make your case together?" Linda's grandfather prompted.

"Well, yes, I guess so, sir." Tad smiled, relieved, feeling he might have an ally.

Chapter Fifteen

After breakfast and the family meeting, and a telephone call from his parents inviting Linda to stay at their home, Tad let Foolish Boy and his sisters lead him for a walk around the hilly countryside behind the Cherokee Phoenix as he awaited the verdict.

Upon their return, Linda emerged on the porch, looking different. Her hair was out of its kerchief and fell like a shimmering dark waterfall past her shoulders. The dig uniform he was used to was replaced by a red-flower print sun dress with gauzy sleeves that fluttered in the slight breeze. One soft leather ballet-style shoe turned inward in the first awkward movement Tad had ever seen from her.

"Am I all right?" she asked. "For Atlanta?"

"You're fine."

Her family emerged behind her. Naomi Tassel wore a bravely congenial smile. Her husband rested his arm on her shoulder in the casual intimacy Tad imagined had been theirs since they were the ages Linda and he were now. Linda's Aunt Theda moved her vehicle toward Tad and placed the remains of their breakfast chestnut loaf into his hands. It had gone down well with the chicory root coffee the family favored and he was glad to have more of it.

Linda's grandparents patted the heads of Foolish Boy and his sisters, one black and one white. Tad waved to them all, feeling honored by their trust.

As they began their trip, the smiling waves stayed on his mind.

"I need to know something," he said quietly.

"What is it, Tad?" Linda asked.

"Was it done enough? To stick? I mean, before I messed up?"

"What are you talking about?"

"Last night. The ceremony…formula, whatever it was that Guli was doing. Do you think your aunt is safe?"

"Nobody's safe, Taddeusz. But, yes, I think it was completed."

"Okay, then."

He put the car into third gear. Soon they were heading for interstate 400 and on their way to Atlanta.

Once they were cruising, Tad started a new topic cautiously. "I think we should talk about Dr. Steffy's death as best we can…rationally."

He felt Linda's frown. "Without Indian superstitions and visions?" she challenged.

Tad winced, remembering his own first, disturbing vision of Linda at Little Mound, buried under an avalanche of red dirt. It had come back, in his dreams. He couldn't ask her about that. What would she think? That he was making fun of her family?

"That's not what I mean," he said evenly.

Linda said nothing.

"Forget it."

"Moses," she offered. "Let's start with Moses."

Tad breathed out, relieved. "Good. A question: how did he get in there with Tallalla?"

"Slid in under the tarp. Whoever killed Dr. Steffy left in a hurry and didn't put all our rocks back in place. That's how Moses got in, maybe, after the killing."

"Yes, you noticed the tarp was altered, didn't you?" Tad remembered. "Do you think Moses was put there? Did he ever escape from his sideshow tank before?"

"Never."

"So, it's likely someone put him there."

"Why would anyone do that?"

"To frighten us away? To kill us?"

"But why?"

"Well, why was Dr. Steffy a target?"

"I don't know!"

"Okay, okay. Let's concede we're not good at the whys."

They drove on in silence for the next couple of minutes. Tad didn't want to bring up the authorities' ideas on why—the Cherokee Coalition, but Linda had gone quiet again.

Maybe he could coax her. "So, if Moses was put in there, who might have done it?"

"I don't know," she said again.

"Linda, those guys from the Cherokee Coalition took credit for it, so the case against them is—"

"Weak."

"Now, how do you figure that?"

"It was only after the news report that they claimed responsibility for transporting Moses down there with their incantations to the Thunder People. Why not before? They had all day to boast."

"I—"

"Because they did not know about Moses until the news report, when everyone else did."

"Hey, you're good at this."

"Thank you. Now, you."

"Me?"

"Come up with a person to consider," she challenged.

"All right. How about Caleb Barker? What was he doing around your site?"

"He was looking for Moses. Foolish Boy brought him to help us."

"Could Caleb Barker have wanted to scare you away from working at the dig? So you'd take the job as his Indian princess?"

"No. He is not a mean man. Mr. Barker just likes to tease me. And did you forget that he's the one who pulled us out of the pit?"

"Part of his plan, to be around in case we got into real trouble."

"That was not real?"

"What's going to happen to his El Dorado Diggings when the dam goes in?"

"It's on high ground. Instead of being a roadside attraction in the middle of nowhere, his attraction will be on the shores of a man-made recreational lake."

"Hmmm."

"Hmmm, what?"

"I'm thinking."

"You should think of someone else, maybe."

"There are plenty," Tad said. "Like all those at the dig site all night."

"Who were sleeping."

"Not everybody."

"What I mean is, we all have alibis as weak at Guli's, don't we?"

"I guess you're right. Bill Steele. Now he seemed different, afterward. Did you know he had kids?"

"No, not until he told us."

"And gambling debts?"

"Gambling debts?"

"Well, I mean, he played poker in town. And he said that Dr. Steffy won big that night."

"I do not think they are high-stake games, Tad."

"Okay, okay, maybe the photographer is a bust. Your turn. Got a name to consider?"

"Dr. Bonaparte Duncan."

"Bonaparte? That IS his name?"

"Be uses B. Wilber Duncan. But Mr. Steele did a computer check at the university. He is wicked that way," she said, holding in a giggle. Good, Tad thought. She is treating this like a game. He wanted to hear her laugh again.

"Well, Bonaparte Duncan. We have our murderer," Tad said as gravely as he could.

Linda turned to him, her hair dancing. "Is that so? And his motive?"

He tried to make his voice nasal and professor-like. "Small man's complex, compounded by name zat was the gift of his cruel parents. Case closed." He sighed. "Still, I can't picture Dr. Duncan sneaking around in the middle of the night in his red silk drawers."

"He doesn't wear…?"

"Scout's honor," Tad assured her.

Now a cascade of giggled erupted. But then she fell silent again.

"Hey," Tad prompted. "Let's keep the suspect list going, we're doing okay."

"No."

"Not even for amateurs?"

"We are not amateurs. We do not love any part of this."

So. Linda knew Latin roots of English, as well as being fluent in Cherokee. He was way outclassed. "All right, then," he admitted. "We're awful at this."

"No. It's Dr. Steffy who makes an awful murder victim. He was not rich or hateful or powerful."

"I hardly knew him, Linda. Maybe it would help me if you told me more about him? If that's not too painful, I mean?"

"I'd like thinking of him," she began, hesitantly. "As alive, instead of how I found him," she whispered, looking down at her hands.

Tad waited. The silences between them were becoming easier, Tad realized. "Did Dr. Steffy have a family?" he asked.

"A brother, who is a farmer in the Midwest." Linda chuckled softly. "I remember him saying they were both in the dirt business. Their parents are both dead, and he never talked about a wife, or partner."

"Did Dr. Steffy ever work with you at Little Mound?"

"He visited. And he was respectful. He always treated me the same as any of the other site supervisors."

"Yeah, he was that way with me, too, respectful, when he sure had no reason to.

Wait a minute. The soil, under Tallalla's rock."

"What about it?"

"Maybe that's why he was there. When Dad and I were sifting it, Dr. Steffy walked over and talked with us. All I could think of when Chief Hawes asked me about my contact with Dr. Steffy was that he praised my observation skills. Well, I wasn't very good about remembering the whole scene."

"What about it?"

"Dr. Steffy said there was something unusual about the soil. The soil from under Tallalla's rock, Linda."

"What did he say? What did he say exactly?"

Tad needed a few seconds of Linda's patience now, as he tried to recreate the time in his head. "He called it interesting, and odd. He asked if you were making the trench opening wider."

"I was not. I would never mix levels."

"I told him that, Linda." Tad took the steering wheel in both hands and concentrated on the memory. "Dr. Steffy asked if it seemed the bones had been disturbed."

"Why did he ask you that? Why not me?"

"I don't know, Linda. What's wrong?"

"He did have doubts about my abilities! He was not what he seemed."

"Maybe he knew you'd be upset. He told Dad and me not to tell anyone about his

151

concerns until he'd checked the soil for himself. Gosh, how did I forget that?"

The silence was thick between them as Tad drove on. Finally, Linda touched his arm. Her fingers were so cold it startled him.

Tad," she began gently. "Did you walk away from the wheelbarrow while I was in with the computers? Did you find buckets from another site and put them together?"

"What do you think I am, some stupid kid?"

"No, but...I have worked so hard. Dr. Steffy could not have been right in his suspicion."

"I'm just telling you what he said. If he was right, what would it mean?"

"It means the integrity of Little Mound has been called into question."

"How?"

"By looters, Tad. Dr. Steffy must have suspected a tunnel, and looters, if the soil does not date from the same period as Tallalla and the mound builders. If it's more recent."

"So that's what he was going to check? He took a soil sample when he told Dad and me to not mention it to you, because it might mean something, or nothing."

"It is nothing," Linda said firmly.

"I wonder where the soil sample is now."

"Chief Hawes did not mention it?"

"No."

Linda breathed a heavy sigh. "Tad, I think the morning he was killed, Dr. Steffy was checking the source of the soil sample. He was taking some soil of his own. That's why he was at Little Mound, alone, so early in the morning."

"Maybe we'd better call the chief. Maybe we should stop and call him right now."

He felt her hand squeeze his forearm. "No."

"Why not?'

"Because this new information makes me a suspect."

"What? How?"

"Think, Tad. Little Mound has been my site since I was fourteen. Everyone knows how I feel about Tallalla. She is like my family. They know I could never divide myself into some rational, scientific acceptance of devastating news…to have her site devalued, after all this time, all this effort and devotion. Someone might think I would do anything to cover up such a discovery."

"But you didn't even know about Dr. Steffy's suspicions until just now."

"I cannot prove that, can I? And they have your mother's news report, with my own words, my own, what did you call it? Enthusiasm coming through."

Tad didn't like the tone Linda's voice was taking. It was as if she was seeing herself getting arrested, being convicted along with Guli, of murder.

"All right," he said, against his better judgement. "We'll look into this ourselves. We'd better head to Current News Network straight off."

Chapter Sixteen

It was a different Linda Tassel that Tad saw reflected in the polished glass of the opulent Current News Network elevator. She looked dazzled and overwhelmed, as out of place in this world as he had been in hers. Tad touched the small of her back as the doors opened on the twelfth-floor lobby with its massive sky lit atrium where a crowd was lining up for a TV studio tour.

"My mom's boss," he said at her ear, "they don't call him Lowman the Showman for nothing, eh?"

Linda smiled uneasily and took his hand. "Tad," she whispered. "We're going to tell this man what he should and should not do?"

"Without getting Mom fired," he reminded her.

"Maybe this is not such a good idea."

"Hey. We've come this far," he said, trying to convince them both. "They're just people."

"People in suits."

"Besides," he said, pointing to the dizzying height of the atrium, "they probably won't let us into the inner sanctum at all."

But to Tad's surprise, they got directed from the general information desk to a separate bank of elevators.

Once off, they kept getting passed from one assistant to another, all of them cheerful and cordial, offering a look at the new sound or editing facility, then a studio for a cooking show, when all he'd asked for was to see his mom.

At one point their paths crossed with an official tour. A woman pointed at Linda and nudged three of her friends.

"Look, do you know if my mom's in the building?" Tad asked their latest guide, a lean young guy in a boxy tan suit.

"Yes, of course. Where else would she be?"

"Out on assignment?"

The assistant stopped before large mahogany double doors. "No. She's in here, in conference. We didn't know how long, so we thought you'd enjoy a VIP look around." He leaned back on a desk, revealing a trendy metallic strip in his suit's vest. As the double doors opened, he came to attention.

Brett Lowman, complete with his Clark Gable mustache and signature flamboyant designer print tie, entered the anteroom.

"Tad Gist!"

Tad had met the man only once, but the media mogul greeted him like a long lost cousin. "And you've brought us the young lady who has caused us to hire a half dozen temp operators to handle our busy phone lines! Come in, come in," he invited, with a slow wink toward Tan Suit. "Perfect timing, Tim."

Once inside, Kelsey Doyle, her shoulders draped in the red scarf Tad remembered she'd always worn when going into battle with her Buffalo bosses, rushed past a gaggle of newsroom executives to take Linda's arm.

"I'm so sorry, Linda," she said. "I was working on the documentary story about the dig, and gave sample footage to Sydney, and he—"

"Insured that your Sunday morning snoozer got upped to primetime documentary. Now it will go through the ratings roof." Tad remembered producer Sydney Perdue as looking angry and out of place at the dig site. Here he looked angry and in place.

Brett Lowman sighed elaborately. "As you can hear, we have spent the morning engaged in the most lively conversation. Though impressed with your mother's coverage of Buffalo's blizzards, we thought we had introduced her to our viewers with a simple, soft news feature. Now we seem to be embroiled in the eye of a tornado."

As Brett Lowman turned his attention to the gaggle of executives around the conference room's oval table, Tad lowered his voice.

"Mom, we need to talk with you. They've taken Linda off the dig. Shut down her site. It isn't right."

"That damned Eyewittness Seven broke that development first," Sidney Perdue shouted from two grey suits away. "It's our story! That's what isn't right!"

"Sit down, Sidney," Brett Lowman demanded in that same polite, molasses-cured pace that everyone respected and no one dared imitate. "Now, I would like to hear what these young people have to say. So I shall allow you jackals to continue formulating your proposed strategies. When I return I will require details and aftermath speculation regarding those strategies."

Brett Lowman opened another set of double doors and directed Tad, his mother, and Linda through. The room beyond boasted spectacular views of Atlanta's skyline with gleaming high-rise buildings of all shapes, some looking like they could fit inside others. The woodwork of the huge office continued the mahogany theme. Walls held framed certificates. Glass encased shelves held trophies and awards for achievements and philanthropy. "Brett Lowman's ego wall spans three counties," his mother had joked after her first day on the job. Tad saw what she'd meant and they exchanged knowing glances.

Linda sat in the plush blue velvet wing chair that Brett Lowman offered with a sweep of his hand. Tad and his mother shared a Victorian style fainting couch. The pieces were all expensive reproductions, made for Americans of the larger twentieth century variety, he observed, almost unconsciously. He'd observed a lot over years of helping his parents haul antiques out of old houses and barns.

Lowman propped himself up against his roll top desk and folded his arms casually. "Now," he said, "Am I right in assuming that you two young ones have lost your positions?"

Linda looked up from the man's snakeskin cowboy boots. She touched the amulet of the necklace Guli had placed over her head last night. Tad had not asked about it, or about what kind of relation a clan brother is. But he was glad that she seemed to draw strength from the gift. "No, sir," she answered. "We were re-assigned."

"Here," Tad continued. "To Atlanta. We'll be processing data." He took a deep breath. "But first we came here to ask you not to broadcast my mom's documentary until the dig is complete."

Lowman leaned forward. "Why?" he asked, drawing out the word as if it had two syllables.

"The Peterson company already has its bulldozers stationed at the dig site, so Morris University's time is running out, Mr. Lowman.

Since the first newscast, Dr. Hamilton has been getting harassment phone calls."

"From whom?"

Linda touched Tad's arm.

"We don't know for sure, sir," he said, obeying her unspoken plea not to mention the Cherokee Coalition.

"The university is caught in the middle, Brett," his mom's no-nonsense voice came to his rescue. "Various environmentalist groups as well as some factions among the Cherokee have always been against the dam. The landowners, Peterson, and local businesses are on the other side. Then Current News stepped on toes because we happened to be on the murder scene first. The police are investigating us all."

"Investigating us for bias, Kelsey?"

"Don't play games, boss." She used the tone of voice that Tad heard when he'd forgotten to unload the dryer, again. "You knew what my husband did for a living when you hired me. I'm a reporter, trying to get at the heart of a story. Chief Hawes respects that. But what am I supposed to say when he informs me that my own producer has lobbied the Georgia legislature for Peterson in his tobacco interests?"

Linda's hand went to her mouth.

Lowman bristled. "That was years ago, before the plans for the dam were even on paper."

"I thought I could trust him with my story. It's Perdue who lit this fire."

Wow, Tad thought. Way to go, Mom.

"How?" he demanded now, in that same soft, intense tone.

"Brett. All I'm saying is that Morris University steps in to try and save some history, and gets battered by both opposing factions. Then a murder. Which may or may not be connected to a three-year feud."

Brett Lowman steepled his fingers under his chin and remained silent.

"How did that happen, Mom? Tad asked her.

"Your father tells me that from the beginning some of the Cherokee feel that Peterson made a deal to gain access to the mounds. Now Peterson thinks the university double crossed him in a last-ditch effort to stop the building of the dam. Newcomers from the North like you and your father are always suspect. And Linda is a bridge person. I'm afraid our spotlight had thrust her in the middle of her two worlds."

Linda smiled for the first time since they'd walked into the building. "I'm used to that position, Ms. Doyle," she said.

"Well, little lady," Brett Lowman drawled out as Tad watched his mom wince, "since this news gathering system got you into your current difficulties, I wish you would allow us to help you out."

"I do not understand you, sir," Linda said.

"I propose we rush the documentary, not delay it."

Tad felt himself failing both Linda and the university. Of course, his face showed it.

"Tad, Tad," Brett Lowman declared now, "Thanks to Current News Network, an obscure university-sponsored archeology site has a good portion of Georgia rallying behind your efforts!"

"Our efforts?"

"To have the dam hearings re-opened! That's the way our phone calls are polling, twelve to one. You've got an ally in Current News Network. And we're big enough to take on any heat. From Peterson, from state and local officials who were perhaps too fast and free about granting him access and damming permission.

"And from the Cherokee," he said more sadly. "I imagine they think of this as one more broken promise, especially since one of them is being held in connection to Dr. Steffy's murder. But I've got an expert coming on in prime time tonight, an expert in Mississippian Culture. He'll make the historic argument, based on what he's seen of your little pipe carver, young lady."

"Tallalla?"

"Exactly, your Tallalla. Very savvy of you to have named her! People love that—Pocahontas, Sacagawea, Minnehaha …Indian heroines, great stuff. Our expert says your Tallalla's work rates up there with

162

the very best of pre-Columbian art. It belongs in a museum, not under water!"

"No sir," Linda exclaimed, her voice shaking. "Tallalla's grave must be remade, reconsecrated. And her work belongs to the Cherokee. The university promised this. After the data and artifacts are collected and processed, Tallalla's work will be given into the care of the Principal People."

Brett Lowman approached his opulent High Victorian chair, throwing Linda into his shadow. "Now, now, I don't know all the details. My overpaid scalawags are supposed to fill me in between now and my two o'clock meeting. Tad, why don't you get this little lady some lunch? I'll have my secretary make a reservation at Chez Nous, on me. Go on, while your mother and I get back to work on all this. And don't worry.

Tad felt like a bothersome child being sent out to play as his mother led them through the conference room.

"I'll insist that you pre-screen the documentary, Linda," Kelsey promised. "I'll keep an eye on Perdue. Maybe he's just looking for ratings. And maybe he's still working for Peterson. I'll find out, even though he knows I'm watching him like a lioness."

Linda smiled. "He does look treed."

Well. Tad grinned. Linda just complimented a woman he didn't think she'd ever talk to again.

Linda sat on the ledge of the luxurious fountain in front of Current News Network headquarters. Tad watched her trace water rippling over stones.

"Tad," she whispered, "I feel so lost."

"Manipulated?"

"That, too."

He leaned over. "Let's cut their strings on us."

She looked up. "All right."

Tad read aloud the note that Brett Lowman's secretary had handed him, addressed to the owner of Chez Nous. "André, please place the lunch of the bearers of this note on my account," it said. Tad looked up and scanned the groups of wandering tourists. He spotted a twelve-member Girl Scout Brownie troop and two tired looking troop leaders.

"Them?" he asked.

Linda smiled. "Yes, them," she agreed.

Tad took her hand. They walked over to the group.

"Pardon me," he said politely to the two women. "Mr. Lowman is delighted that you came to visit today. He would like you all be his guests at lunch."

"Well, that's very kind of him, but we've brought our brown bag lunches. Tad handed her the note and gestured to Chez Nous across the Current News Network Square.

Her eyes brightened.

"Atlanta Troop 1951!" she exclaimed in a fulsome voice. "Brown bags in packs! Pull up your socks! Merit sashes facing forward! We have a chance to earn our etiquette patch this afternoon! We are dining at Chez Nous!"

Tad heard Linda's soft giggle as the little girls and their leaders marched off, waving.

"The bill might shock Mr. Lowman," she said. "Even I don't eat as much as a troop of hungry Brownie Scouts."

Tad shrugged. "That's done. Now, I have eight dollars. Where would you like to have lunch?"

"Home," she said. "Yours."

Chapter Seventeen

Maggie was playing in a maze she'd made of moving van boxes. When Tad pulled into the driveway, she burst through a flapped window like a curly topped jack-in-the-box and ran toward him. He wondered when she would outgrow that habit. Not soon, he hoped.

He got out of the car and opened his arms for her hug, then lifted her high. His father came out on the porch and waved.

Maggie's blue eyes squinted as Tad introduced her to Linda. "Do you like dragons?" she wanted to know.

"Sure."

"Want to visit mine? It's dangerous."

"Oh, I'm sure it will be worth it."

Tad left Linda crawling behind his little sister through the box maze that led to her lair. After helping his father prepare lunch, he returned with clinking glasses of sweet tea, grilled cheese sandwiches, and a fruit bowl.

As they all sat together on the wide porch that faced the Atlanta skyline, Tad noticed more of the uneasiness in Linda's manner.

Even in their quiet neighborhood, she seemed overwhelmed with sights and sounds Tad had grown up with—a plane on its way to Hartsfield, an impatient taxi honk, the clamor of neighbors' conversation.

Her eyes seemed to find refuge in the leaves of the front yard's mountain laurel and dogwood trees. That was a nice thing about his parents' passion for old neighborhoods, Tad thought. Their houses usually came nestled in vegetation planted so long ago that house and greenery fit together like old friends.

"What's your favorite animal?" Maggie asked. bringing Linda out of her reverie.

"The wolf," she replied. Tad wondered if she was missing Foolish Boy.

"Wow. This will be interesting," Maggie said, running off, Tad knew, to find her crayons and drawing paper to construct one of her hybrid animals.

This time it would be a wolf-dragon, for Linda.

Tad picked an apple from the fruit bowl and turned to his father. "Did Mom interview Peterson for her documentary?" he asked.

"She tried to, but he's reclusive. She couldn't even find a photograph taken in the last twenty years. And you know how persistent your mother is. Doing down-the-rabbit-hole research is how she found out that her own producer, Perdue, had worked for him.

Tad's father's culinary skills couldn't approach Mrs. Christie's, but Linda complimented their lunch before suggesting that she and Tad start their data entry duties at the university.

"Tomorrow will be soon enough for that," Dr. Gist insisted. "You two have had a harrowing couple of days. You need some down time. Why not take in the Age of Exploration exhibit at the High Museum?"

"Can I go with you?" Maggie begged in her most please-please-please voice as she jumped into Tad's lap.

Most of his girlfriends were annoyed at Maggie's devotion. But Linda was laughing.

"Sure, Sprite. Why don't you help Linda get settled in the guest room? I'll do my chores and we can be off."

Tad wanted to get his clothes in the wash before his mother got home. He loaded the machine and turned it on. After a moment he heard the dull thunk of something hitting the metal drum. He opened the lid and poked around. His jeans, the ones he'd been wearing on the first day at the dig site. They were still smudged with dirt from his aborted attempt to seal third base during the softball game. They bore bloodstains from when he'd lifted Linda out of the dig site the next day, too.

He reached into the right front pocket and pulled out a clump of clay— the one he'd picked out of the sifter while working it with his father.

That clump had started everything, Tad realized with a shock of discovery.

It was made of soil from the level of Little Mound the Dr. Steffy had wanted to study. Tad held it up to the light streaming through the laundry room's window. Something was visible through the dirt. A dull yellow color, embedded.

Linda didn't need to know about this yet. Especially since it was something his addled brain had forgotten. What if it proved to be nothing? And they were on down time, weren't they?

But had his reluctance to show it to Dr. Steffy contributed to the man losing his life?

"Tad! We're all set, where are you?" his sister called.

Tad felt a surge of energy. Maybe they could find some answers to this nightmare. He put his find into his pocket.

Chapter Eighteen

Tad parked in the museum's underground garage. Over their heads, he heard the dull rumble of thunder.

"It can't rain," Maggie said. "Linda has to see the dragon at the 'Tanical Gardens after we're done!"

Linda smiled. "I do not mind the rain."

"Wow, Tad! None of your girlfriend's don't mind being rained on!" she marveled.

"Maggie," Tad warned.

"Look at me, I'm Julie Tolliver!" his sister proclaimed, with a dead-on imitation of her fussing over her wet hair.

Linda giggled as Tad locked up the car. "The bane of little sisters," he said with a sigh.

The truth was, he never thought he'd hear Linda's musical laughter in this city. He didn't even mind that it was at the expense of an old girlfriend.

Old girlfriend. Is that what Julie Tolliver was now? Linda didn't ask about her. And he didn't ask her about Guli Whitepath. How did she feel about the guy she danced with in that beautiful cape her grandmother made? What was a clan brother, exactly?

They were both being polite. Sometimes he hated polite.

The Age of Exploration exhibit was a popular one, they discovered as they entered under an archway leading to an exhibit called "Martin's Hundred—Tidewater, Virginia." A clever behind-glass miniature of an archeological excavation similar to their own was the first stop.

Tad found counterparts in clay for all their own workmates, even a grey-haired lady in khaki offering some diggers a bowl of fruit.

"Mrs. Christie!" Linda proclaimed.

"You know that doll lady's name?" Maggie asked.

Linda laughed, then told Maggie about their dig, using the model. Her voice was full of fondness and passion. Maggie listened, wide-eyed.

Tad wondered if the murder and its enhanced publicity had put them all behind glass, like the display. He stepped back further, then further, watching Linda bend down so her head was close to Maggie's. An eerie feeling that they were going to become part of the display visited.

That's when he stumbled into the man.

He nodded when Tad apologized. "You look like you belong in there," he said, his quiet words echoing what he was feeling about Linda and Maggie. Even slightly stooped, the man had an understated elegance, from his unnaturally smooth, almost stretched skin, to his sharply creased slacks, to his highly polished shoes. Tad looked down at his own scuffed boots. Why hadn't he changed them? Fear of snakes, even here within the marbled halls of High Museum?

"I've been working at a dig site."

"Really?" The man smiled, showing imperfect, stained teeth, a chink in his best-of-everything appearance. Was he afraid of dentists? "Then don't bother with that diorama for school children. Let me show you something really interesting."

Tad looked toward Maggie and Linda, their heads still together. enjoying the display. Well, how long could it take? He followed the man further into the exhibit.

The lighting was different, more subdued, its display cases showing the ground plan of an old Virginia fort, with traces of its original wooden foundation. Tad noted the room's displays of polished armor and helmets, dull gold coins, a wrist cuff, and other jewelry.

"The remains of Wolstenhome Towne, Martin's Hundred," the man said. "Established 1619, burned to the ground 1622. A massacre. But it has yielded this treasure. These are the earliest colonial

American pieces known. But the conquistadors were here a century before these lazy English planters. They came right up to the hills above Atlanta, did you know that?"

"Yes, sir."

"Of course you do. De Soto's expedition is part of your local history."

Tad wasn't going to tell the man he wasn't a local Georgian, that he'd learned about de Soto from Caleb Barker. This soft-spoken stranger wanted something, Tad felt sure. He looked around. The room had emptied of visitors.

The man took hold of his arm. "Look at the pounding this breastplate took. The armor didn't save him from the savages. It didn't save De Soto's party, either, who were not stupid farmers, but adventurers, in search of the fabled cities of gold. Imagine holding that armor in your hands, full of the spirit of those men! That would be a find far surpassing than anything at Martin's Hundred, wouldn't you say?"

"I wouldn't know, sir."

"Why? You must think about these things. Consider what side you're on."

"Side?"

"What is the purpose of archeology? That is what you must decide if you remain in the field. Is it a splendid treasure hunt for those of us who can feel the power of our heroic ancestors? Or Is it to be left in the

173

hands of corrupt governments pretending to be guardians? They are only trying to stay in power with presenting displays for bored schoolchildren."

"Is that right?" Tad tried the phrase his dad used when he wanted to get away from a conversation. Next part of the strategy: try to pivot the discussion. "Are you a collector, sir?"

"I am. Did you know that ours is one of the few countries where private ownership of historical artifacts is still permitted?"

"No, I didn't."

"It's a sacred right, that some would trample. Stupid, superstitious people who call private collectors looters, yet let locals charge fifty cents to visit trumped up fake tombs of the conquistadors!"

This meeting had been planned. He had to get out, away.

"I'd better find my sister and my friend. Excuse me, sir."

"Wait."

He kept moving.

"Tad, wait."

But Tad was already rushing through, trying to find his way out of the now darkened exhibit. He didn't stop until he spotted Linda, dwarfed by a huge statue of Christopher Columbus with his hand on a globe.

"Tad! Where were you? A man told us those rooms were closed for the rest of the day due to a private showing. He ushered us all away. When we asked for you, he said you'd gone out another way. Isn't that strange?"

"Was he a guard? Was he wearing a uniform?"

"No. A suit."

"Where's Maggie?"

"In the gift shop. Buying you a present. I'm not supposed to peek. Tad, what's wrong?"

There. Maggie, at the cash resister. "We have to go."

"Why? What happened?"

But he was already sprinting toward his sister.

"Tad!" Maggie protested, when he grabbed her hand.

"Hey, Sprite. Show me my present."

Maggie clutched her paper bag tighter.

"How about at the botanical gardens?"

"Today? Now?"

"Sure, let's hurry, I can't wait," he said, pulling them both towards the exit.

"I'll tell you when we get there," he assured Linda.

Chapter Nineteen

A summer storm had drenched the city while they were inside the museum. Tad watched its black clouds heading north over the head of the whimsical dragon topiary that framed the entrance of the botanical gardens.

He felt himself relax in the brightness of the rain-freshened day. Linda's company and his little sister's enthusiasm helped, too. They walked together through the park's Japanese gardens. They took a winding trail through a hardwood forest before settling beside a pond.

Linda peeled the oranges that Tad's father had packed for them while Maggie presented Tad with a comb studded with bits of polished stone.

"You can keep it in your pocket, see? Mom says you might use one more often now that you work with Linda."

"Did she?" Tad frowned. "You can tell Mom that Linda likes my hair just the way it is."

"Do you, Linda?" Maggie asked.

"Oh, yes," Linda assured her.

"I want to visit Tallalla," Maggie said, taking the orange sections Linda offered. "I want to help at your dig."

Tad reached into his pocket. "Here's one of Tallalla's secrets, still hidden in the dirt." He offered.

Her eyes opened wide when he put the clump in her hands. "What is it?"

"Now if I knew, it wouldn't be a secret."

Linda leaned in. Maggie made a face. "You're teasing. It's just dirt."

"Might be. But Tallalla's given Linda many treasures. Would you like to see if anything's inside?"

"Sure!"

Linda spread out the paper towels that had been holding their orange slices. Maggie set down the clump and Linda began chipping away the red clay with her blunt-tipped fingernails. Tad thought of Julie Tolliver's long, perfectly manicured nails. Julie would never be doing what Linda was showing Maggie with such enthusiasm.

"It's treasure! A pirate coin!" Maggie proclaimed.

"What are you smiling at? Help us!" Linda demanded of him.

"Hmm… needs to be categorized," Tad told them. "Remember the spigot we passed in the Japanese garden, Sprite?"

"Sure."

Linda smiled. "Find a bird's feather on the forest floor. Use its quill point and the flowing water to get the coin as clean as you can."

"And when I do?"

"Bring it to us and we can talk about what you found," Tad promised.

"Over ice cream," Linda finished.

They watched Maggie skip down the wooded path with her treasure. Tad felt Linda's hand at his shoulder.

"I like the kind of brother you are."

"She makes it easy. Linda, I need to know about Guli."

"Guli? What about your disappearing act at the museum?"

"Do you have feelings for him?"

"Of course. He's my clan brother."

"What does that mean?"

"Distant relative. There are seven clans left in the Cherokee nation. We call each other brother and sister and never refuse a clan member shelter. That's how Guli knew he would be welcome at our home when he came to perform the ceremony." She paused. "We are forbidden to marry anyone in our clan group, as we share grandmothers, even long ago ones." A small smile crept over her face, "Of course."

"Of course," Tad said, knowing he was turning red as he spoke. "So, you wouldn't like, go out with him or anything?"

She laughed. "Is that what you wanted to know?"

"Well, he kissed you!"

"Like a brother. Not like how you and I have kissed." She shook her head. "You Buffalo people can talk around a subject. *Ayh wah*, so polite!"

They laughed together and Tad felt better. Much better.

"You will tell me what happened at the museum now?" she asked.

"Sure. But now that we're out in the air, in the daylight, it seems less strange. Maybe you'll think I'm crazy."

"The whole exhibit seemed a little crazy to me."

"Meaning...?"

"Well, dead."

"That's some statement, coming from a friend of Tallalla."

"I do not think of Tallalla as dead," Linda said quietly. "Part of her spirit remains in her burial chamber. She speaks. That morning, Foolish Boy was listening. We were not. At the museum, they separate artifacts, divide them, and the sense of them, the sense of the whole community is lost. I hope the Cherokee will do better when the artifacts of the Mound Builders are returned to us." She made a small, disgusted snort. "Did you see? They even sealed us living people off in clay and plaster, on display. Is that part of what you felt?"

"Yes, something like that. Linda, did you see that old guy? The one with white hair and expensive clothes?"

"No. Maybe I was too busy explaining the people in the diorama to Maggie. What did he say to you, Tad? What did he say to make you so shaken when you came out?"

"At first I thought he was fishing for information. About me. About the dig."

"The dig?"

Tad rubbed his forehead impatiently. "Maybe not the dig. Why would I think that? He kept comparing the artifacts from the Virginia exhibit to those that might come from de Soto's march up into the Georgia hill country. He said the Spanish expedition was more important than the English settlement."

"Because they were looking for gold? He sounds like Mr. Barker."

"Yeah. He seemed to know Caleb Barker too."

"Know him?"

"Knows that he charges fifty cents to get into his de Soto cave, anyway. He hated that. Too undignified, I guess, because de Soto is a personal hero of the guy."

"You two had quite a talk. What is his name?"

"He never said." He took her hands. "But Linda, I never did either. I never introduced myself."

She smiled. "I will not report you to Miss Manners."

"You don't understand. He called me by my name."

"Maybe he heard one of us talking with you."

"Yeah. Maybe. But Linda, this guy was slick, smooth, but, I don't know how to say it, with an edge. I didn't want to tell him anything. Especially about you."

"Me?"

"Because he spoke of 'savages' like he was in some old western movie. But I did say I was with my sister and a friend. Why did I do that? Why couldn't I let him think I was alone?"

"Are you afraid for us, Tad?"

"Yes," he admitted. "Stupid, isn't it?"

Then they heard Maggie's scream.

Chapter Twenty

Tad could feel the blood pumping through his ears as he ran.

He sensed Linda behind him but he could only look ahead at the small form lying beneath the water fountain. Maggie as so still he thought his heart would stop.

He went to his knees and touched her shoulder gently, calling her name. She turned slowly, then leapt into his arms, almost knocking him over.

"He pushed me down, Tad!" she cried, her voice ringing in indignation as she buried her head in his shirt. "That man took the gold quarter and pushed me down!"

Tad cleared the curls from his sister's forehead. There was a scrape over her right eye. Linda wet the hem of he skirt in the water, then bathed the dirt around it. Maggie smiled. "That smells like you, Linda," she said.

The bruise around the scrape wasn't swelling, Tad realized, breathing easier.

"Let the sun see you, Maggie," Linda coaxed gently.

Maggie obeyed, blinking, as Linda studied her eyes. "Dilating," she said. "Her pupils are dilating."

No sign of concussion.

Tad took his sister's arms gently. "You were so still, Maggie."

"Playing possum. Like I did when Mrs. Craighead's dog got free and jumped on me after school, remember? I didn't like that man. I was almost finished cleaning the quarter, and I tried to hold onto it. But he bent my fingers back. It hurt!"

"Let me see, Sprite," Tad urged, taking the small hand and feeling the joints of each finger. "Anything still hurt?"

"No."

"Good," Tad said gruffly.

He took his sister into his lap the way he used to when she was smaller. She still fit. Her arms circled his neck. She rested her head on his shoulder. Linda turned off the water spigot and rejoined them.

"Why did the man want the quarter?" Maggie whispered.

"Quarter?"

"That's what I found, under the dirt. A quarter. But not like one of ours. It was gold, and a funny shape, like a pie. I saw part of a head, and writing, and numbers. A two and a seven. I kept the water running. I was just starting to work on the other side. That's why I didn't hear the man, I guess."

"Did he say anything, Maggie?" Linda asked.

"No. He took in a breath, and grabbled. 'Hey!' I yelled, 'Let go, that's Tallalla's!' Then he pushed me down and ran away."

"What did he look like?"

"Mean. I'll draw a picture of him. Of the quarter, too. Can we go home now, Tad?"

"All right, Sprite."

"Linda, too?"

"I'll keep a good hold on both of you."

* * *

Tad watched them from the doorway of Maggie's bedroom. Linda reached behind her neck and transferred her stringed amulet to his sister.

"What is it?" she asked.

"Campion root. The Cherokee call it 'snake's master.' It will help to protect you from further harm."

"But what will protect you?"

Maggie looked up at the doorway, noticing Tad. Linda made room for him on Maggie's small bed.

"Mom told me about the snake. Were you scared?" she asked them both.

"I was," Tad said.

"But his fear did not stop him from helping me," Linda said. "Just as it did not stop you from making your drawings of the man, and Tallalla's coin."

"Will that man come after me?"

"I don't think so. I think he has everything he wanted."

"And I bet he doesn't know I'm a good artist! I bet he doesn't think can draw at all!"

"I am sure you are right."

"Will you marry Tad, Linda?"

Tad let out a sound that was half a snort and half a sigh. He hoped Linda knew how little sisters could be.

"I am too young to get married."

"Maybe later? Maybe when I'm in Mrs. Dickinson's class?"

"Fifth grade," Tad translated.

"In four years? Yes, I would consider it then."

"Good." Maggie yawned. "I can wait. I'm very patient, Daddy says. Mom, too. And Tad only sometimes gets mad when—"

"I'm the impatient one in those times," Tad said, staring into the swirling pattern in Maggie's blanket. "I should always—"

"Shh, Tad," Linda alerted him. "She is asleep."

Quietly, they left Maggie's room. Tad turned to Linda in the darkness. "Everything will be all right," he whispered, weaving the silky strands of hair through his fingers.

"Why would someone hurt a child for a souvenir coin?"

"It, ah, wasn't a souvenir."

"You did not embed a toy in the dirt for your sister?"

"No. It was from under the tomb. It was Tallalla's quarter all right."

"You removed it from the dig?"

"Yeah."

"Tad, what you did is strictly forbidden."

"I know. I forgot I had it in my pocket, and then, with everything that followed—"

"Why did you not tell me?"

"You had your hands full. And we were so happy that Maggie was all right, and I just wanted to get her home."

"They were watching her. They still are." Linda shivered.

Tad pulled her close against his chest. "Maybe you're right maybe they have everything they want and will leave us alone. But Linda, this is too big for us. We should call Chief Hawes."

"If only we had something more substantial. A who, what, why."

"You must be tired. You're sounding like me."

They joined Tad's parents in his father's study, where they were huddled over his father's computer screen. His mom pointed to a tray beside them.

"Hot coffee and banana bread," she said.

"Research food," Tad explained, as he poured two cups from the carafe of steaming, cinnamon-flavored coffee.

Linda smiled. "Just like home."

In the dimly lit room, she looked as tired as he felt. He hoped the coffee would revive them. Tad handed her a slice of banana bread as they turned to the graphics on the screen. "Coins, historic" was the heading. Before them was a dizzying array of heads of monarchs.

"There," his mother said.

His father stopped the flow of graphics at a coin bearing the head of the Holy Roman Emperor Charles the Fifth. "His chin," Kelsey said. "Isn't that the one Maggie drew?"

The only Holy Roman Emperor Tad's weary mind could come up with was Charlemagne. Charlemagne in Georgia? This was making no sense to him at all.

"Let's get his brief," his mother suggested.

His father punched a few keys and Holy Roman Emperor Charles the Fifth was identified as the monarch who was also Charles the First of Spain, the Hapsburg grandson of Ferdinand and Isabella.

"Columbus's Isabella?" Linda asked.

"The same lady," Tad's father confirmed. "Her grandson took the Spanish throne in 1516 and the Hold Roman Empire in 1519. A busy guy."

"Now our question is: how did he end up where you found him?" Kelsey asked.

"Dr. Steffy was right," Linda whispered.

"About what?" Tad asked her.

"The coin came from newer soil, I think. Five hundred years after Tallalla. Contact time."

"Tunneled into the tomb? Looters?" Stan Gist asked.

"No, not looters. Everything in Tallalla's resting place was intact. It was the Cherokee, I think, Dr. Gist. Tunneling to her for protection. From the Spanish."

"The Spanish?"

"De Soto," Linda explained. "Hernando de Soto and his army. Mr. Barker knows more about them than I do. For about a generation, around 1540, the Spanish conquistadors were on a mission to find gold fields. Maybe they left behind some of their own gold coins."

"In trade?" Dr. Gist asked.

"Or after the soldiers' deaths, by disease or warfare. They were here for years. The Cherokee people were not fond of their less than polite guests. The woman Mr. Barker wanted me to impersonate for his show…the one the old Spanish records call the Indian queen or princess, she led the Spanish into these hills until they were lost, and then she escaped them."

Dr. Gist took up Linda's idea. "The Cherokee, because of their wide-reaching trading network, knew what powerful enemies the Spanish were. If soldiers were killed, or even died of natural means, they had good reason to fear retribution."

"Fear enough to bury conquistadors among their revered ancestors?" Kelsey Doyle asked.

Linda nodded. "And then circle the site with booger masks, signifying that strangers were within, among the ancient ones. The Mound Builders could be trusted with secrets. They had kept their own for so long."

"Dr. Steffy was putting this all together— the old and newer soil, what might lie within," Tad said. "He was digging under Tallalla's resting stone. He was killed before he could get any closer."

"We're getting somewhere," Kelsey encouraged them. "Would this fit in with Chief Hawes's ideas about a shadow dig?"

"Shadow dig, Mom?"

"Yes. He said you gave him the idea, Tad, when you told him about the local grocer. The bills suggest the town was feeding a large number of people who never showed themselves."

"Our food was coming in from the university's agricultural food co-op, remember?" Stan said. "So the grocer was feeding a shadow dig, maybe working at night."

"If this coin is from a sixteenth century discovery, who would want to keep it a secret?" his mom asked.

There was a long silence.

"Thieves," Tad said.

"Tad?"

"Mom, the man I met at the High Museum today is a thief. He called himself a private collector, but he is a thief. That's why he gave me the willies. He hired the guy who hurt Maggie, I know it."

"But he'd have to know you had the coin, son. Even you didn't know you had it."

"Yeah, he had to know. From the beginning."

The four of them sat in silence for a long time, the flickering image of the Emperor Charles presiding over the room's nervous gloom.

"We've got to get back under Little Mound," Dr. Gist declared. If we find more evidence of newer soil, and a tunnel, a tunnel containing Spanish artifacts…but we have to be careful. There's someone on the inside, working with your thief, Tad, almost certainly. Someone at the dig."

"Dad. The computer. It's part of the university network, isn't it? Can someone find out that we've been researching the coin tonight?"

Dr. Gist's fingers flew. "I'm putting it under a password now."

"I have got to get back," Linda said, her voice ringing with a quiet intensity. "I have to get back to Tallalla."

"You don't mean tonight, do you?" Kelsey asked.

"Yes, tonight. Please."

"But it's almost midnight, and you're both exhausted," Tad's father argued. "Tad can drive you back first thing in the morning, promise."

Tad thought Linda was holding back tears of frustration, but she pressed her lips together. "Excuse me," she said quietly. I am not used to drinking coffee."

Tad remembered the scent of her family's chicory root concoction. But Linda wasn't giving up that easily, he knew her well enough to be sure of that.

* * *

Once his father had switched off the computer and everyone had said their good nights, Tad went to his room. He didn't even take off his boots as he propped himself up high on his bed's pillows.

He picked up the phone from his night table and searched through his scattered belongings for the card with Chief Hawes' phone number on it.

He punched the buttons and waited. A woman's sleepy voice answered.

"I'm sorry to call so late, Ma'am," he began quickly. "I'm Tad Gist. I worked at the Morris University dig site."

"Why, yes. My husband spoke of you. I'm sorry. There's nothing W. C. or any of the local police can do for you now."

"Ma'am?"

"Peterson's done it all legally, I'm afraid."

"Done what, Mrs. Hawes?"

"Shut down the dig. Haven't you been evicted?"

"I'm in Atlanta."

"That's where W.C. is, too. Following some leads, he said, a paper trail. If W.C. had been at the site, he might have been able to call in a few favors, gotten a delay at least. Rotten luck."

"Yeah."

"Dig members were so busy packing up, the university might not have been informed until recently. Do you want W.C.'s phone number in Atlanta?"

"No, ma'am."

"But he said to make sure—"

"Thanks, anyway. There's no need."

Tad sat back, shaking. What had he done?

Connections. Make connections. A university dig in a sleepy Georgia hill town had spawned a murder. The local police chief used to be a bigger fish, in Atlanta. Was he connected to rich looters of the past, feeding their obsessions? Could those looters buy a police chief?

The air became so still that Tad thought he could hear the whirring of his own thoughts. Then he saw the glint of the old hammered copper doorknob of his bedroom turning.

Linda entered his room soundlessly. She crept to the jacket he'd hung over the room's armchair. Her hand was in the side pocket when he folded his arms.

"The keys are on the dresser," he said.

Chapter Twenty-One

Linda's voice was a furious whisper. "Tad! You're spying on me!"

He sprang to her side. "Wait a minute. Who was going to steal whose car?"

She shrank back. "I was only going to borrow it."

"It's standard transmission, remember?"

"I was driving my grandfather's tractor since I was ten, Buffalo Man."

Tad frowned. "Yeah, but... you'd never find your way out of Atlanta, country girl."

"Ellis east to Piedmont, north to seventy-five past the Perimeter and out."

"Okay, I'm impressed."

He handed her the keys, then slouched into his jacket. "You drive. I'll just nap in the back seat."

The anger left her face. "Tad," she said softly. "One of us in trouble is enough. Your parents—"

"I'll leave them a note. We're only getting an early start. Let's call it pre-dawn?"

Linda bowed her head so low all he could see was the spiraling crown of her shining black hair. "Hey. That was supposed to be funny."

She didn't move a muscle.

"Not a night person?"

She shrugged. "I guess not."

"Your grandfather told me as much. And I should know these things. I'm falling hard for you Ahyoka."

She laughed softly. "All I have brought you is trouble."

"Intrigue," he whispered into hair that smelled like fresh rain. "Let's call it intrigue."

He reached across to his dresser where her grandfather's booger mask rested, and took it under his arm.

As they passed the Perimeter highway, leaving the lights of Atlanta behind, Tad noticed Linda's fingers easing their grip on the steering wheel of his old Mercedes. Her right hand touched the empty space at her neck.

"Why did you give your charm to Maggie?" he asked.

"I wanted to make her feel strong and protected."

"Is that what Guli wanted for you? Why he came to perform that ritual?"

She glanced at him quickly before her eyes returned to the winding stretch of I-75. "Yes. He felt badly about the snake."

"Because he killed it?"

"No! Of course not!"

Tad felt the wall between their cultures rise higher. Great going, he thought. Really delicate. He listened to her measured, deliberate breathing. He was surprised when he felt her hand cover his.

"Guli gave me the campion root so that the relatives of the injured snake would not pursue me. The people behind what is happening at the dig, they have many relatives too, I think. I do not want any of them to find Maggie."

Did she notice them too, Tad thought, the two men in the blue Ford sedan that had been within sight since Piedmont Street? He wouldn't mention them yet. They were one or two cars behind, not trying to run them off the road.

Tad took a deep breath. Better stick to real dangers. They were hard enough to talk about. "Linda, did you recognize the man in the drawing Maggie made? Of the guy who knocked her down? A big guy, with dark hair?"

"Your sister did not say he was a native man. Or that his skin was like mine. No one I know would hurt a child, Tad. Not for any reason. Let's talk about your Brett Lowman."

"He's not anybody's Brett Lowman."

"He hired Sidney Perdue, your mother's producer, who used to work for Mr. Peterson."

"Lowman just smells a story. My mom would know—"

"Know? How badly did she want her new job?"

"What are you saying?"

"And what about your father? We never considered him in our list of suspects. He was sifting the soil with you when Dr. Steffy made his observations."

"Are you saying—"

"You see what this circling around does? It makes us suspect everyone, our families, our friends, even each other! That is why we must go back."

Tad nodded. "Because someone saw me pocket that clump of dirt. Is that what started all this? Is an excavation team member a murderer?"

"That's not why we are going back. We are going back because Tallalla knows. Only Tallalla."

Tad looked out at the dark, empty night. He saw Tallalla's bones again, and Linda shielding them, and the world caving in. He shook his head.

"The fuel gauge is low," she said abruptly. She pulled the Mercedes off the exit where the twenty-four-hour gas station was.

Tad looked behind them for the blue Ford. It hadn't followed them off the ramp. He sighed out his relief. Good thing he hadn't voiced his suspicions. He'd said enough ill-chosen words for one night, even for him.

He filled the tank under the glaring white lights while Linda went to the ladies' room. He was paying the cashier when she emerged, looking different. Tired, maybe?

"Are you all right, Linda?"

"Yes," she replied as she brushed past him.

He shoved his change into his pocket and caught up with her. "If you'll navigate, I'd like to drive the rest of the way."

"All right," she said softly, opening the passenger side door.

Well. That was easy. Too easy. Inside the car, he looked over at her. Slouched down in the seat, she was hiding the side of her face with her hand.

She'd been crying, Tad finally realized.

He put the car in first gear and drove just out of the gas station's glare, pulling into a parking spot. He cut the engine.

"What are you doing?" she asked. "What's wrong?"

"Us," he said quietly. "We can do better than this, can't we?" He held out his hand.

She took it, squeezed, and nodded. There. Better already.

"Please tell me what's on your mind."

"We are who they want now, Tad," she said softly. "Because we have stumbled onto their gold trail."

"Gold?"

"Yes. It must be the gold again. Your people are mad for it."

Tad felt his jaw clench. "My people?"

"I mean in the tide of our history, your people and mine, since contact time. Gold, greed, stealing. I do not mean you, personally."

Tad ran his hand through his hair. "What about your parents?"

Her fierce eyes softened. "My parents are exceptions."

"Are we exceptions too?"

She looked out the car's front windshield. "*Ta ka no hi: li,*" she said softly.

"Hey," Tad called her back, smiling. "That's your grandfather's trick. Can't fool me twice. In English, please."

Linda shook her head. "I said, 'we are flying in the same direction.'"

Slowly, Tad reached behind her head. He massaged the back of her neck gently. "*Wa to*, Ahyoka," he thanked her.

She leaned into the massage."*Kv: ke: yu:?*"

Tad continued his caress, loving the feel of her skin against his fingers and waiting for a translation. She didn't offer one. "Will I have to ask your family what that means?"

"If you can remember it."

"Oh, I'll remember it."

Tad leaned across the stick shift and pressed his lips to hers. Their kiss deepened. He felt those strong, capable fingers of hers weave through his hair. He sighed, wishing the car was an automatic.

Chapter Twenty-Two

Tad turned onto I-75. Only an eighteen-wheel truck was behind them now. He breathed easier.

"We should stop and pick up Foolish Boy, maybe," Linda said.

"Show up at your house in the middle of the night, again? I don't think your folks are that polite."

"We will not wake anyone, just get Foolish Boy."

"Why?"

"For company."

"Don't you like my company?"

"Of course. And your instincts are almost as good."

"As a dog's? Thanks."

"You're welcome. I'll let you know the first turn. Let's talk about the mole."

"Mole?"

"You know, inside operator."

"Well, listen to Detective Columbo."

"Columbo?"

"He's a TV detective."

"We do not have a TV, remember? But we all read."

"Let me guess." Tad remembered scanning her living room bookshelves. "Tony Hillerman?"

"And his Diné policemen? Yeah, those stories are great. But I'm trying to think like Jean Hager's Molly Bearpaw. She's Western Cherokee. The ones who went to Oklahoma?"

"I remember."

"Good. Now, let's work on our own mole. "Who saw you steal that clump of dirt with the artifact inside?"

"I didn't steal—"

"Borrow, then."

"It wasn't that either. Linda, I forgot I even had it!"

"Ah, the truth."

"Why are you giving me such a hard time?"

"I'm your supervisor. It's my job. Besides, you are cute when you are angry. Puts a little color in your cheeks. I never knew the meaning of 'pale face' until you came into my life, Taddeusz."

He growled. "And now arguing with you is putting a strain on my heart."

"No changes are necessary there. It is my favorite part of you."

"Linda, what are you doing?"

The teasing tone left her voice, but the nervous energy remained. "I am trying to keep you awake in the dead of the night. I am hiding my fear that your parents will think ill of me for leaving. I am hating that your sister got hurt. I am wondering which of my friends is a murderer. Take your pick, Tad. I am doing all these things."

Tad reached over and touched her cheek with his knuckle. "Hey," he said quietly. "Don't worry. I'm a night person, remember?"

She yawned. "One of our many incompatibilities."

"The mole," he prompted. "Everybody at the dig walked by as Dad and I sifted."

"Not me. I was inside at the computer, remember?"

"Okay, you're in the clear."

"Thank you."

"Linda, what about Mrs. Christie? She was going through my clothes."

"Why?"

"That night. The clump of dirt was in my pocket. I discovered her in my place inside the tent that light, looking for dirty clothes to wash, she said. Was she looking for the coin?"

Linda shook her head. "No, she does that for all of us. And she knew you were two days in those clothes."

"You're very confident. And you reason pretty well when you're half asleep," he teased.

"Dream time. It is for creation."

"Not creation. Reason. You reason on the opposite side of your brain than the creative side."

"I do?"

"Everybody does."

"'Everybody does.' White people talk." She snuggled against his chest.

"Linda," he warned her reluctantly when he realized she'd released her seatbelt to get that close. "This isn't safe."

She murmured something in Cherokee that sounded like an insult, though she also made it sound sexy, as she tucked up her legs and rested her head on his thigh.

"Hey, hey. Wake up, little Suzie."

"I am not Suzie," she murmured from his lap.

"It's a song."

"Oh?"

"Everly Brothers, nineteen-fifties. Before your time."

"Dark ages, Buffalo Man."

"You dust thousands-of-year-old artifacts, and I'm in the Dark Ages?"

"Sing me the song."

He did. By the time he got to the part about Suzie's reputation being shot after falling asleep at a drive-in movie, he was wide awake and scanning his rear-view mirror for signs of the Ford. But Linda was sound asleep.

Who knew "wake Up Little Suzie" was a lullaby? In the silent darkness, Tad enjoyed the feel of Linda's warmth, her scent, her body curled against him. He stroked her hair before glancing at the mirror again.

The blue Ford was directly behind them.

"Linda," he summoned. "Put on your seatbelt. We've got to ditch these guys."

She bolted up. "Guys? What guys?"

"Behind us."

She looked up at the mirror. "Since when?" she asked, adjusting her shoulder strap.

"Atlanta."

"Tad! Why didn't you tell me?"

"Got any ideas?"

"We should not go to my home. Too remote. We should head straight for the dig. I will tell Foolish Boy to meet us there."

"Agreed. Wait, you'll what?"

"Never mind. I think he is already there."

"Linda—"

"Oh, turn off your half a brain and get off at the next exit. I know these backroads."

Tad groaned, but nodded. "I'll enter from the far lane. Fast, to try to make them overshoot. Ready?"

"Yes. The exit ramp is a wide curve, it is inclined."

"Good." Tad took the Mercedes up to seventy, confident that the old car could handle it, and the abuse he was about to put it through. The blue Ford matched his speed, staying close behind. As Tad approached the exit, he did not signal. He barely even turned his head, not wanting to alert the driver behind him.

He relied instead on Linda's calm instructions. "Half mile…quarter…and, now."

He turned the wheel, cutting across two lanes, then a triangle of grass, to the ramp. He only tapped the brake lightly as he drove up.

Behind them, they heard the tires of the Ford screech to a frustrated halt.

Tad breathed easier and risked a quick look at Linda. She was smiling. He ran the stop sign at the end of the ramp.

"Five," she announced.

"Five?"

"Moving violations, in the last twenty seconds."

"I wonder if they give medals for that kind of record."

"Tickets."

"Yeah, well. Where's a cop when you need one?"

He felt her smile. "Tad, Do you think we should have called Chief Hawes?"

"I did."

"When?"

"Before we left."

"So, he knows—"

"He wasn't home. His wife said he'd driven down to Atlanta. That spooked me, Linda. Like he was one step ahead of us. I wondered if he always was."

"But he was so kind."

"Yeah, with me too. When he wasn't calling me a Yankee outsider."

"I do that, Buffalo Man."

"Not the same. It's like everyone has two faces. I don't know what to believe, or who to trust. Oh, maybe I should have told you this before. Peterson has shut down the site."

"Drive faster," she said.

Chapter Twenty-Three

Nothing could have prepared them for what they saw. A brilliant glow in the northern sky. It came from high-powered, industrial lights.

It was as if there was a city in the distance.

Tad slowed the car before turning into the road to the university dig site. The parking area was reassuringly the same, though more crowded than Tad had ever seen it.

"I don't recognize any of these cars," Linda said as they pulled into a spot on the grassy plain. "Could all the university people and equipment be cleared out already?"

"I don't know. But something is here."

"Something big," Linda agreed.

Tad got out of the car and took Linda's hand as they climbed the hill that led to the site.

It was as if the Peterson Company had constructed a city since they'd been gone. Barbed wire stretched around the site and checkpoints manned by security guards were everywhere. The dig itself was flooded with light, the kind of light like at the gas station. The din of generators and the roar of earth movers were a deafening intrusion on the north Georgia night. Only the university's white trailer looked familiar.

Linda broke their stunned silence. "It is like a dream. A terrible dream."

"Stay here," Tad urged. "I will—"

"No. They are finished with us. They are finished talking."

He took her arms. "Please, Linda. Let me find out what's going on. Wait for me, back at the car."

"No." She pressed her lips together.

"I'll find you, I promise. And if I don't show, you can get help."

She nodded curtly, tears in her eyes, and walked away.

Tad felt strange facing the white trailer's door without her. The structure was now part of the barb-wired circle around the dig site.

A man exited, his broad shoulders straining the grey private security firm uniform shirt as he put a cap on his head.

"Stop right there," he demanded. "Who are you?"

"Tad Gist. I'm with Morris University."

"When are you people going to take no for an answer? We gave you as much time as we could to clear out. You can't keep coming by for stray beads and pots."

"I was sent to Atlanta. I didn't know about all this."

"Look, don't take it up with me, kid. I'm just maintaining security so these damned Indians don't try anything. If you ask me, it's you people who stirred them up!"

"How's that?"

"Putting them and their ancestors up on a pedestal like they were kings or pharaohs! This ain't Egypt. It's north Georgia hill country, never good for anything after the gold played out. Mr. Peterson's putting in a lake. That makes jobs, brings Atlanta people up here. Fast food, motels, that's progress. Damned Cherokee don't understand progress. They killed the professor, then the TV gets into the act and Mr. Peterson gets pushed into strong arm stuff."

"If I could just—"

"Ain't you listening to me, boy? That damned dog's got me riled enough, don't test my patience."

"Dog?"

"Yeah. Got inside, been spooking our drivers at the sites Mr. Peterson wants filled in first."

"Little Mound."

"I don't know what you call it." He gestured vaguely. "We took a few shots at him, but he disappears in the brush."

"I know that dog, sir," Tad said evenly. "Maybe I could leash him for you."

The guard raised an eyebrow. "Why would you do that?"

"He belongs to a friend. Maybe he's looking for her. We'd hate to see him hurt. He's a good dog, sir."

"Well." The man rubbed his chin. Would speed things up if we could get a hold on that animal. I'll check with Mr. Peterson."

"Mr. Peterson is here?"

"Yep. The big man himself, right here in command center. Beats me which one he is. His bodyguards all look like him." He pointed back to the white trailer. "Must have smelled a court order coming from the Indian lawyers of the kid they're holding for the murder. Figured he'd go on and exercise his rights to the land first."

"But he promised the university—"

"Like I told you, he gave those university people a couple of hours to sack up their loot and get out. They're a bunch of grave robbers. Now, if you're still willing to help with that dog—"

Tad looked over the man's broad shoulder as they both turned. The door to the trailer opened.

An entourage of men emerged. The guard was right, they all had a similar look. But only their boss had the rich man's buffed face.

The conquistador admirer from the museum.

The guard turned. "Kid?" he called out. "Hey, kid, where are you?"

Tad watched his flashlight's beam scan the rhododendron bush he had ducked behind. When it passed, he bolted for the outskirts of the glaring lights. He had to get to Linda.

He ran for the car. She was gone.

He thought of the sad, desperate look on her face when he'd left her. She was getting to Tallalla her own way. If there was a hole in Peterson's defense line, she'd find it.

How could he find her?

He rummaged through the car's emergency supplies, pulling out a flashlight, screwdriver, tie-downs, matches, and safety flares. He stuffed them into his backpack, along with the Cherokee booger mask Linda's grandfather had made. Then he headed down to the river.

As he walked, Tad kept listening for the sound of the Allatoona's flow. The thicket grew less dense. The moon came out from behind clouds to show him the winding river's trail. He followed the rocky shoreline until he found the place where he'd met Linda after his mother's news report appeared on television.

She wasn't there.

Tad heard the rumble of the earth movers getting louder. Had she reached Tallalla?

Maybe he could slip under the barbed wire. Nothing in his backpack would cut through it, but the bungee cord might help him rig up the wire so he could slip under it. He pulled out the cords, clipped the ends to the wire, then stretched it over to the nearest post. Yes. A wedge opening appeared.

He sent his backpack through. If he could fit his head and shoulders, the rest of him would make it.

Now or never.

A gusty wind shook the rolled wire. Tad didn't like the idea of looking up at the sharp barbs, but being nose to the ground had even less appeal. He flattened himself to the ground and began shimmying through the opening.

He'd sneaked into a few closed basketball courts in Buffalo like this. Piece of cake. Razor cake.

His head and neck cleared before he took his first breath. Shoulders, there. He could move more quickly when his arms were free to grab the kudzu vines on the other side.

Tad looked down at his legs. The wind gusted. Razor wire cut through the tie-down, snapping it in half.

Tad scrambled. One leg free, but he wasn't fast enough with the other. He heard the sickening slice of a dozen barbs cutting through his jeans and into the flesh below his left knee.

Tad's instincts screamed for him to struggle, to do anything to get the wire off him. But he knew that to obey those instincts would only lead to further injury, maybe even cut through a tendon. He fell back on his elbows, trying to think through the pain that was making him grind his teeth.

Then, suddenly, the awful, cutting weight was lifted.

"Well, scoot, boy," a familiar voice commanded, "I can't hold this forever."

Tad scrambled out from under the wire to see Caleb Barker, and his heavy leather work gloves releasing the blood splattered wire.

"Mr. Barker—"

"I know, son. Peterson's men caught us all off guard. But I got something on them now. I found what they are stashing. It was right under our Linda's site."

Tad caught his breath. "You found it through one of your tunnels. Signs of de Soto and his men."

"That's right! How did you—"

"Linda's there, Mr. Barker. At Little Mound. I've got to get her out."

Tad rose to his feet. As he reached for his backpack, purple spots appeared before his eyes. He missed the handles twice before securing his hold.

"You all right? You don't look so good. There's a bunch over at El Dorado Diggings, playing poker. I'll get us help. Stay here."

"I can't. I've got to get to Linda. They're filling in Little Mound. Foolish Boy is here too. They're shooting at him. I've got to get them out."

"All right, all right. Stubborn Yankee. Tell Linda to go down, dig down, you hear? I'll get help, meet you there."

Tad pulled on his backpack as he watched Caleb Barker disappear into the dark night. He turned toward Little Mound and the sound of the bulldozers.

His left leg hurt. It felt heavier than the other, impeding his speed. But he could move.

What kind of help was coming? Tad imagined the poker game. Faces he's come to know over the past few days appeared. Dr. Hamilton smiled, revealing vampire's teeth. Mrs. Christie had Tad's clothes in her lap. She searched through his pockets, her angelic Glinda face turned suddenly wicked. Dr. La Vetra offered Tad sun block that was bubbling acid, burning his leg. Bill Steele looked about desperately for his poker winnings, and his children. Dr. Duncan rose, thumbing over his shoulder to call Tad out. And Chief Hawes snapped handcuffs, not on Guli's wrists, but Tad's.

Tad shook the images out of his head and tried to concentrate on one thought: find Linda.

One of his boots seemed heavier than the other. Why was that? Then his left leg crumpled beneath him.

A dry tongue swiped Tad's face. He heard a familiar whine of concern.

"Hello, Foolish Boy," he said, rubbing around the hard bone at the top of the dog's head. "They're after you, you know."

Foolish Boy growled softly.

Tad noticed the torn cloth between the dog's teeth. "Looks like you've been after them too."

He stroked behind the dog's ears. The touch made Foolish Boy open his jaws in a wide yawn. Tad got a better look at the remnants of brown tweed and beneath it, shredded red silk.

Tad rose to his feet and limped the remaining way to Little Mound, Foolish Boy at his side. Tobacco smoke wafted up through the light shining on Tallalla's stone bier. The ancient bones looked beautiful to him, for the first time.

Linda's head appeared from beneath the stone.

"You done?" he whispered.

"Done." She reached up her hand. Now, are you two going to chat the night away, or help me out?"

The gun's blast roared in his ears. Tad fell to his knees before the weight of Foolish Boy catapulted them both into the trench.

Then darkness came.

Chapter Twenty-Four

Linda looked down at him.

No, that's not right, Tad thought. Wasn't he just looking down at her? He was in Tallalla's place, on her bier. And the pit was shaking under the earthmover's power.

Tad bolted up. "Linda, get out."

She shook her head, saying something, that Cherokee phrase, the one she'd said in the car, and refused to put into English.

The din was so loud.

He looked above. Dirt began to rain on them.

"I love you," he said.

She nodded, smiling through her tears. "Good translation, Buffalo Man."

Linda leaned over him protectively. It was just like his dream, or vision, or whatever it was, except this time he was not looking down at a tragedy.

He was in it.

Then the walls buckled and the earth came tumbling down.

Chapter Twenty-Five

Tad grabbed Linda's arm and pulled her underneath Tallalla's stone. It provided a breathing space as the earth came down.

"Foolish Boy!" Linda summoned with a small cry in her voice. Then louder.

She was rewarded with a low whine that sounded somehow far away. Tad yanked his backpack from his shoulder, found his flashlight and flicked it on. Linda was on her knees, digging, calling her dog.

"Here," Tad said, handing her what he found next: her grandfather's booger mask.

"Help me, Tad."

He grabbed the screwdriver, loosening the clay dirt. "Yes. Mr. Barker said to dig down."

The whine came again. From below. There. They kept digging, burrowing, following the corkscrew passage the dog had made. Widening the hole, shoving themselves through.

Foolish Boy's whine was louder, and now had an echo. Or was he hearing things?

Then he felt a breeze. Tad thought he must be dreaming. Dreaming or dying. Linda pulled his arms.

"Come on." she urged, coughing.

Don't talk, he wanted to tell her, there isn't enough air to talk.

But, suddenly, there was.

Foolish Boy barked. Tad lifted his head. Space. Air. Even some light.

The tunnel they forged had opened up into a rock-faced cave.

Linda helped Tad through the opening. She eased him down slowly along the glistening wall, then sat beside him on the ground.

Tad swept the small underground chamber with the beam from his flashlight.

Armor and weapons that had served their wearers as they searched for cities of gold were neatly stacked and tagged along the walls. The room was a storage chamber for another dig, the one that was a shadow of Morris University's. Or maybe the university's dig was the shadow of this one. Tad thought of Peterson and his smooth, unnatural face. his greedy eyes.

Tad's leg burned, above the cuts from the razor wire. What had hit him? He remembered a blast. Shotgun fire? Whatever it was, Linda's dog had taken more of it.

"Where's Foolish Boy?" The rough, dry, exhausted sound of his own voice surprised him.

"Looking for a way out." She swept the hair from his eyes. "He will come back for us."

She handed him her grandfather's booger mask. "Your talisman was very useful, Buffalo Man. What else did you bring?"

"Some stuff from the car emergency kit that my parents insisted I carry. And I complained about."

"A man who listens to his elders. I am gifted in my companion." She took the flashlight from his hands and shone it in his eyes. His fall. She was worried about him and checking his eyes, as she had Maggie's. She moved on, feeling his shoulders and along his arms.

"I'm all right." He tried to steer her away from his leg, as much as he enjoyed her gentle probing.

"Hey," he remembered, "We love each other."

She grunted softly and went back to searching his backpack.

"Wish I'd brought water, I'm so thirsty."

She held up the flares.

"Not edible," he apologized.

Linda's laugh had a nervous edge. "Tad. You're bleeding."

Busted. "Not serious," he said.

But his leg was throbbing, and he felt hot, and their crazy surroundings felt vague and dreamlike.

He felt her cold hands take hold of his face. "Foolish Boy will find the way out. He will bring help."

Tad nodded. "I told Mr. Barker I went to get you. He said to dig down. How did he know there was a tunnel beneath Tallalla's tomb?"

"Because he was a meddlesome man."

Tad felt fear strike a surge of adrenaline through his system.

Linda stood. "Dr, Duncan. "I'm so glad—" But her sentence snapped short when she saw the revolver in his hand.

Chapter Twenty-Six

Dr. Duncan was between them and the passageway beyond. "You should not have come back, Linda," he said in that same voice he used at their end-of-day assemblies. "I didn't want to hurt anyone. But you are so persistent. You are all so persistent."

Tad touched Linda's back. "In Foolish Boy's teeth. Red underwear. Silk."

"And why shouldn't I have a few comforts after all my years of toil and trouble?" Dr. Duncan demanded. "Do you know how many dig sites I've supervised? For how many universities?"

"No, sir," Linda said quietly. "We don't."

"Mayan ruins in Guatemala. Tombs of the Inca in Peru—hammered gold puma heads with teeth of polished seashells. I supervised, drove off pistol-packing looters, corrupt customs agents, greedy collectors and their deep pocketed agents. Was I ever more than a footnote, more than a 'with additional thanks to' in their books?"

"Dr. Duncan—"

"Never!" he cut Tad short. "So I wanted out, that's all. I wanted to retire in some comfort, a reward from that idiot crazy for the conquistadors. I'll take that money, I thought. For once, I'll take something for myself. Let Peterson have his armor, his private shrine to de Soto. He's no better than that cracker Barker was."

"Was?" Linda whispered, as she dropped to her knees beside Tad.

"I had to! He wouldn't have taken money to shut up. After all these years in this business I know the scavengers, and the ones too honest for their own good. Well, Barker became another casualty of his Legend of the Lost Boy's well."

Linda's small cry echoed off the rock wall.

"As for Steffy. He should have left you on your own with your pipe carver's tomb. Stopped looking for assistants. You were getting too close. You were already too close to where the booger masks were buried, to keep the Spanish away from their ancient ones."

Tad looked up to Duncan's face. "Caleb Barker allowed you to explore his caves, before the dig got underway. How could you kill him?" he demanded, trying to sound indignant, and not what he was. Desperate, and trying to buy time.

"Ah, he told you about my unauthorized preliminaries, did he? When I saw you two with him, I worried, but just for a moment. What did his friendship with a couple of kids matter? Now I'm sorry I underestimated you two. And his knowledge of these old gold mining shafts.

"I told them that this far in they were Peterson's property now. He should have stayed out of the way. He was all set to profit from the dam, wasn't he?"

"He knew?" Linda asked softly. "Caleb Barker knew about you selling the Spanish artifacts to Peterson?"

"He didn't know anything until you and your questions! They started him exploring some of his own. That first year, when we found the booger masks guarding the whole site. I had an inkling that there was more to be found. That's when my independent operation began. Generously funded, of course. We were all set to profit.

"But you had to work so hard, Linda. On the edge. Not dissuaded by your own people's activists. I didn't know how close you were to breaking through to the tunnel until I heard Steffy talk about the soil from your site, that looked younger."

He narrowed his eyes. "And then I saw you pocket that gold piece," he directed at Tad.

"You knew that piece of clay had gold in it?"

Dr. Duncan laughed. "I haven't been in this business for thirty years without knowing what gold looks like. Steffy had to be dealt with first. I also knew how to make it look ritual. If that huckster hadn't rescued you from his snake, it would have been perfect. Slicing him up only made you all more determined."

Tad felt Linda shiver beside him. Keep him talking. "The coin was in my pocket, I never even saw it."

"Never saw it?"

There, he was intrigued.

"How did you know you have a Charles V gold piece in that soil sample?"

Linda rescued him with a question of her own. "How did you find out?" she challenged, her voice hoarse with fear. "Dr. Gist had it sealed under a password."

"Too late. I was on line as you began your search. But how did you know what you had?"

"My sister drew us a picture of the head on the coin." Tad said. She saw it, if only for a moment."

"Your sister? That little girl?"

"Yes, that little girl who your henchman terrorized." Tad couldn't keep his voice calm when he thought about Maggie.

"That part was out of my hands," Duncan said gruffly. "If it hadn't been for that damned dog guarding you. I had no opportunity to get the soil sample or the coin. Then came your mother with her new clothes, her gold foil truffles, her disruptions! The whole scheme's

224

gone out of control since you and your family started meddling! I've worked it carefully for two years, without anyone getting hurt. You tore it down in days! You've been an expensive lesson to me, Tad."

The dig administrator's eyes now focused on Linda in the dim light. The softer tone he used somehow scared Tad more. "I liked you, Linda, he said. "I only meant to scare you away from your site with that snake. I thought the boy would go down first, with those low, prep school shoes. It should have bitten him, you see? It would have stopped there, if you'd let him go down the ladder before you. But you had to be his boss. I'm sorry it's come to this. You were the only one who never called me Bonaparte."

He motioned impatiently with his gun. "Get up, both of you."

"He can't," Linda said.

"What?"

"Tad can't get up. He's hurt."

"I hit him?"

"Yes, sir." Linda yanked Tad's head down on her shoulder. "I think he's passing out."

Tad closed his eyes dutifully as he felt the flashlight survey his face.

"I don't want to shoot you," Dr. Duncan said quietly. "Not up close. The look on Steffy's face. All because he wouldn't turn around! A fall down a mine shaft. That will be easier on all of us, won't it?"

"Yes, sir. We can walk, can't we, Tad?"

"I—"

Linda shook his jaw in her cold hand, turning the rest of his objection into garble. She looked up at the man with the gun. "He's lost blood. Maybe I can bring him around with some of the chocolate bar he's got in his pack."

"Choc—?" Tad started, but again Linda shook his jaw. Harder, this time. Now he really was getting dizzy.

"Yes, yes, try that." Dr. Duncan looked behind him. "Hurry up."

Linda turned her back on Dr. Duncan. Tad opened his eyes, amazed by the calm serenity he saw in hers.

She rifled through his backpack. He nodded, finally understanding what she was up to. She put the flare in his hands. "Come on, Tad," she urged, "smell the chocolate."

That would be his job. To light the flare. If he could do that there would be a blinding light, then a dense smoke cover. Tad eyed the passageway, maybe five feet away, curving left.

That was their way out.

Could he get up? Would his legs hold him? They'd better. Both their survival depended on it, because Linda had already proven that she would not leave him to save herself.

Linda picked up her grandfather's booger mask, holding it like a frisbee. Ah, her part in the plan. Tad thought of her prowess on the softball field.

He smiled, wanting to tell her he had every confidence in her.

She grinned, as if he had.

He'd have to be fast. She would have to be accurate.

"Take the chocolate, Tad," she said.

Tad struck the flare to its flint base. He heard it ignite just as Linda whipped her lithe body around and pitched the mask at Dr. Duncan.

A startled grunt was her reward in the sudden, glaring light, the smoky blaze of the flare.

Linda grabbed Tad's hand. He scrambled to his feet, leaning on the rock wall.

"What the hell?" Tad heard Duncan exclaim. The shot echoed off the wall. Linda made a soft, surprised grunt before her grip on Tad sprang loose.

Tad called her name, but the ringing in his ears was so loud he couldn't hear his own voice. He swung around in the dense white smoke and hit a rock wall.

There, the soft feel of Linda's sleeve. He grabbed hold and ran, limping, his heart pumping hard, his eyes swelling and tearing.

But he was still anchored to Linda, though his grasp was growing slippery with sweat. No, not sweat, he realized.

"Linda—"

"My throwing arm. It felt like a bee's sting."

Then, she screamed.

Tad's forward momentum crashed them both into Caleb Barker's embrace. Foolish Boy licked Linda's hand.

"Easy, you two!" Caleb said. "Your hound and I are still recovering from being tossed into the safety net under Lost Boy's Well."

Chapter Twenty-Seven

Tad's eyes were shut underneath the cool cloth. He figured he'd swallowed down about a gallon of Mrs. Christie's lemonade. He couldn't remember anything ever tasting as good.

"Academics are not known for being world class shooters," the little woman said. "A good thing for the two of you."

"Three," Linda corrected as Foolish Boy whined softly between them. The paramedic tied the last stretch of gauze around the dog's hind end. Tad's suspicions had been right. Foolish Boy had taken most of the shotgun's pellets that had also scattered into his leg. He felt around for the dog's boney head and rubbed hard.

He peeked out from the wet cloth that covered his eyes. He was grateful that Dr. La Vera and Mrs. Christie had kept up the card game tradition and were on hand to come in with the paramedics and police to treat their injuries. He saw the blur of emergency vehicle lights.

And in their midst, a blue Ford.

He lay back again.

"You are one crazy driver, son," W.C. Hawes said, above him.

Tad moved, but the police chief's hand held him down.

"That was you following us, sir?"

"And a deputy. Doc says a shotgun and some razor wire got to you before us. Ambulance ride to the hospital to be checked over and out soon. All the parents will meet you there. How do you feel?"

"Stupid. For not trusting you."

Linda squeezed Tad's hand. "Will you release Guli Whitepath, Chief Hawes?" she asked.

"With our apologies."

Tad heard Caleb Barker's drawl join their conversation. "Do you think he'll be too ornery over all this to dance with you when the dig site is preserved, Linda?"

"Preserved?" Tad asked.

"Sure, now that the burial ground of de Soto's famous lost expedition has been discovered. It beats anything for an early contact find."

It was not dug in that way," Linda said. "It was dug in haste. To keep the ancestors safe."

"Missy, those conquistador gold seekers didn't have the integrity of what was in your Tallalla's little finger, we both know that. Maybe they got what was coming to them all these centuries later—having their armor trussed up and sold to the highest bidder. But now it's too important to flood."

"Why, Mr. Barker. Be careful with such opinions. The Cherokee might consider adopting you."

"Scoot," Dr. La Vetra commanded as she lifted the cloth from Tad's eyes, smiling.

Mrs. Christie touched his arm. "I'll leave a plate of blondies. Don't feed them to Foolish Boy."

"No, Ma'am," he promised.

Tad watched them all walk away, except for Linda and her dog.

She brought the freshened wash cloth to his eyes. "Close."

"But I can see now."

"Final rinse."

"Maybe you shouldn't be using that arm yet."

"Dr. La Vetra says the bullet did not hit bone, and barely touched muscle. "That is how it could keep... ricocheting."

Enough to enter and leave Dr. Duncan's body twice, and the second time pierce his heart. The emergency workers who found his body had come up with that theory.

With Dr. Duncan dead, would the police ever find enough evidence to link the Peterson company with criminal activity, Tad wondered. Was the rich developer already buying off informants, destroying all links that led to him? Tad could picture Peterson explaining calmly that he is a private collector respecting the privacy of his supplier, and of course antiquities may be owned privately.

Tad wanted to revel in the joy of being alive after the past few days, so he drove his worries from his mind. He removed the cloth from his eyes and stared at Linda's bandaged arm.

"Only a graze," she reminded him. "I don't even have a bullet fragment to raise my status in my clan," she groused.

"What have I got? Razor barbs and bird shot. I might as well have been a crazed cow."

Linda peered into the metal dish of barbs and pellets swimming in bloodied disinfectant. Tad didn't know any girl who would do that with such interest.

"You could call it shrapnel," she suggested.

"Shrapnel? Yeah. I like the sound of that. Want some?"

"Uh, sure," she said, imitating his Buffalo accent to perfection.

The End

Eileen Charbonneau's stories explore the perspectives of people often left out of history: women, first peoples and immigrants, marginalized poor.

Eileen has published fiction for adult as well for young readers. She lives in the brave little state of Vermont with her husband Ed. She adores him, her kids and sweet grandchild. Eileen is addicted to reading, watching great movies, exploring her beautiful state, country and world, roots music and dance of all cultures, and Vermont maple creemies. (write to her at eileencharbonneau@gmail.com and she'll tell you what they are!) Eileen loves to hear from readers. You can find her at:

https://bookswelove.net/charbonneau-eileen/
eileencharbonneau.com
email: eileencharbonneau@gmail.com
twitter: @EileenC1988
Facebook: Eileen Charbonneau Author
Instagram: eileencharbonneau
Blogs: http://manituwak.blogspot.com
https://bwlauthors.blogspot.com

BWL Publishing

bwlpublishing.ca